When Alan Morgan, a world countless distances from the planet of his birth, he had only his intelligence and his masterful swordplay to keep him alive. Llarn was a world of uncharted deserts where cities of incredible age lay broken and empty, destroyed long ago in the great War which had scourged the planet. Those few cities which remained, and those blue and golden skinned people whose ancestors had lived through the War, gave a coldly hostile welcome to the strange newcomer.

But before long he had met the lovely Tuarra, princess of Kharthol, and he vowed he would fight his way across the entire planet to win her—against the savage swordsmen, the fierce beasts of this world, and even against the immortal radiation-being which had brought him here for its own unfathomable purpose.

WARRIOR OF LLARN

Gardner F. Fox

ACE BOOKS, INC.

1120 Avenue of the Americas

New York, N.Y. 10036

CHAPTER ONE

*C*ome to me, man of Earth! I call! I call!

The sweat was wet upon my body as I sat up in bed, eyes wide. I saw the wood panels of my hunting lodge bedroom, the silver of a moonshaft tinting the quilted rug on the floor and the bureau drawer handles.

It is almost time. Soon, now. Soon. . . .

The clock on the bed table told me it was close to five o'clock. Nearly time to get out of bed, if I wanted to get that wolf. The air was cold and my breath made wisps of fog before my lips.

In my mind the echo of that alien voice still lingered. This was not the first time I had heard it, nor even the hundredth. It had come to me ever since I can remember, first as a small child, then as a youth and now—as a man. It was an old friend.

And yet—

It had been so long since it had called to me across the void and the eons, from whatever place in space and time it occupied. I had come close to forgetting all about it. I shivered and slid back under the heavy covers, not sleepy, just puzzled.

Soon now, it had said.

The time was come for—what?

What did the voice want of me? What mission was I to go on for this being whose mind was so incredibly powerful it could bypass the barriers of the space-time continuum to find and summon me? I lay there and tried to think, to go over what part the voice played in my life, its meaning and its inexorable hold on my body and my mind.

All my life I have heard the voice.

It was no more than a whisper in the dim recesses of my mind at first, while I was a small child. A purr of pleasure at being with me, at having—found me. In the years that followed its first appearance, the whisper became a part of my very being, as if it were a lonely animal discovering a friend. Never did it frighten me, not even in those early years when it came strongest between waking and sleeping.

Never did the voice call me by name. Not once did it say Alan Morgan, nor did it acknowledge the life that occupied my waking hours. Having found me, it was content merely to be with me. Already the voice regarded me as its own; its property, in a manner of speaking. I was too young then, too filled with childish fantasies, to put up any opposition.

I say a voice, because I know no other way to describe what it was that touched my mind at such an early age. With maturity, I understood that the voice had never spoken to me, other than with flashes of its own thought processes. I sensed an emotion of satisfaction, of pleasure, and also the fact that after many failures, it had succeeded in some sort of quest.

I was the third and youngest son of a prosperous Middle West lawyer. There was nothing about me to suggest a reason why I should be singled out for—owning. I went to the right schools as I grew older, played the right sports; I even went two years to a military academy where I learned the use of firearms and became something of an expert with the foil, epee and saber, an ability I continued even after my college years, as some men continue with their squash or handball.

Somehow I sensed that the voice was studying me as I grew to manhood, as if it were a part of me in a sort of symbolic existence which set me apart—in my own eyes, at least—from the world about me. It became like a conscience inside me, forcing me to study, to exercise, to adopt certain mannerisms and habits which became ingrained in me as a way of life. Perhaps it guided me, through the use of its peculiar properties, along a path which it laid out for my feet to follow.

I did not fight it. I enjoyed everything I did at its subconscious bidding. I was a novice studying a role I was to play in later life, or so it seemed at the time.

Though Earth is the planet of my birth, it held no allegiance from me as a human being. I felt that I belonged to another place and another time; I was here on Earth only because the laws of happenstance—a scientist might call it the theory of probability—had ordained it.

Such was the teaching of the voice.

And yet—

There were times when the voice went away and stayed far beyond my plane of existence for as long as a year, though rarely more than a few months. Once having found me, I was not to be let go, like a prodigal strayed and now, in a manner of speaking, on his way home.

I was filled, toward the last, with a sense of waiting. I was now a man, in my late twenties and in the full strength of mind and body toward which I had been guided, with a few hobbies, such as collecting old swords and learning their use, at which I excelled through natural ability, and with a flair for the outdoor life. I wanted no four walls around me, only the open woods or the salt spray of the ocean in my face.

I loved to hunt and fish, far more than any other member of my family, and we were all great sportsmen. In the weekends when I could get away from the law practice to which I had fallen heir by reason of my birth, together with my brothers, I fled into the woods. I must admit that I was never the lawyer my father and brothers were; to my mind the law seemed dull and uninteresting. I would far rather fight a twelve pound steelhead in the tidewaters of Big River or trail a bull moose through the Minnesota wilderness than sit through the most notorious murder trial.

In the wilds of the northern country, I could feel the voice more clearly inside me. The loneliness of the wind whispering between the pine branches, the crunch of pine needles underfoot, all were conducive to its coming.

I understood that someday the voice would summon me to it, to whatever world it called home, for a purpose which it had planned long, long ago, far back in time before my birth. It had hunted the star worlds for other men like myself, in ages past. I was merely its latest choice—to do what it thought must be done to . . .

My thoughts always became chaotic at this point. Either my mind could not grasp the thoughts poured into it or the voice-being never bothered to tell me what it was I must do for it. I was its servant—the latest in a long line—and it was desperately hoping that I would be the man who would achieve the goal it set me.

A little of my future it gave me, in my dreams.

It showed me unreal visions, glimpses of what was to come. I stood naked and alone on a great red desert in those dreams and ahead of me was a shimmering pinkness toward which I must run and run. Something in the pinkness was of the utmost importance to me and to the voice. Always I woke before I came to the pinkness, in a sweat of terror.

There were other scenes, too, from the mind of the voice-being. I hovered in the air above a great metropolis that was old, old, though filled with men and women like myself, however differently garbed. I fled across ancient sea bottoms and dallied above the waves of an ocean that ran thinly and without force in these last years of its existence. I saw ruins of yet more cities, dead and pallid like old bones in the moonlight, and caught glimpses of men with blue skins.

These were not complete dreams but mere flashes of light and color, as though the voice-being called to me from far, far away and across a great gulf of emptiness. Yet each revelation was dear to me, held hungrily to my mind and heart because I knew that someday I would see the reality of what was only a dream at the moment.

I was hunting, as I say. The family owns a cabin in the Goose Island country, an expensive bit of redwood and plate glass, with all the modern conveniences. My father bought it as a retreat where he could study his appeal briefs and trial minutes; his sons had taken it over. For me especially, it had become a second home.

I loved its stained gun racks, the mounted deerheads and painted decoys on shelves in the big living room, its grey-stone fireplaces—a huge one in the living room, smaller versions in each of the five bedrooms—and the view of the woods from almost anywhere on the porch that borders the house on every side. This was a minor heaven in my eyes, for it was here, far from the crowded, hot city, that I received my most vivid dreams and heard most clearly the calling of the voice.

Of late, a big grey wolf had been terrorizing the houses in the valley below, raiding the chicken coops and runs, frightening the children, once even killing two of the town dogs in a running battle. My heart went out to the big lobo, for something in my nature responded to the wild, the unconquered; yet it had to be destroyed. This corner of Earth was grown too civilized to be long the prey of a timber wolf. And so I would have my sport and do the villagers a good turn at the same time.

I selected a Remington 721 for the job. It was a lightweight gun and easy to maneuver in the brush if I had to snap off a shot in a hurry. I filled the leather pocket of my hunting jacket with brass-jackets and set out through the mists of early morning.

I had not yet eaten breakfast. I wanted no food smells about me as I slipped between the tree boles. Long ago I had come upon a narrow trail through these woods, too small to be made by a man or deer; I was willing to bet money that my lobo came by this path down into the valley and then back into the high hills. The cold frost was on the leaves and in my nostrils. I was vitally alive, so that my blood seemed to sing in my veins. I was promising myself a plentiful helping of flapjacks and sausages when—

I froze.

Alan Morgan! I cannot seize you! You are too—alive!

It was the voice. Troubled and frightened and desperate with urgency! I froze stockstill, to listen. And into that intense silence I heard the brush of fur against a low hanging twig, merely the bare whisper of a sound; yet my every sense was attuned to it.

Instinct makes a man perform acts without his consciousness being aware of them. The Remington was at my shoulder, the barrel steadying as my eye lined up grey fur against the vee sight. My finger squeezed. All this, even as I heard the voice crying out to me, almost wailing its despair.

The gun bucked. Flame ran from its muzzle.

The wolf leaped high, kicking. It was snarling and I knew that I had not given it its death wound. It flipped in midair and came down with all four paws scrambling at the ground. Then it was leaping for me.

Saliva dripped from red lips backdrawn in a snarl, baring huge white fangs. Green eyes gloated on me as its prey. The hunter had become the hunted, all in an instant of human error. The wolf lifted upward at me, forepaws outstretched, sharp fangs cleared for slashing. My gun went up. I struck with the darkly grained stock, felt the clamp of teeth on an arm and went down. . . .

I lay on my back under a huge, hot sun.

The rough grate of sand was under my naked skin, and as I rose to an elbow and stared around me, I knew a moment of utter terror. The woods and the wolf, the early morning frost and the Remington 21: where were they? Where was I, for that matter? I came to my feet, staring at my forearm. There were bloody streaks where fangs had entered my flesh, and blood welled up where the skin was torn.

I looked from my arm to the desert where I stood. It was vast, vast, stretching on for endless miles to where this world curved at its horizon. I turned in a complete circle. Nowhere was there anything but desert. And a big red sun, up above me, baking me and this sand as though I stood inside an oven.

It was not a disagreeable heat for it was dry and I was—naked. Nothing remained of my hunting jacket, my heavy leather shoes, my canvas slacks, except the memory. Like the wolf and the Remington, my clothes were somewhere far behind me.

I stood and waited for the voice.

It did not come. It was if, by delivering me here to this desert, it had accomplished its purpose. The rest, apparently, was up to me.

I was still hungry. I remembered the flapjacks and sausages I had not eaten for breakfast and my mouth watered, reminding me that I was thirsty, as well. There was no place to eat or drink on these sands. I would have to go someplace else for that, quite obviously.

I began to walk.

As I strode along, I noticed that my body seemed to be stronger, my step lighter than it was on Earth, here on this strange new world. I had no way to account for this extra vitality at the moment. I accepted it as I accepted the fact that I was no longer on the planet of my birth.

This planet was somewhat smaller, I assumed, and its gravity less than that of Earth. My muscles, developed on the planet of my birth, gave me an added agility here. I remembered that the voice-being had told me it had brought others to this planet in the past; I wondered if they too, were from larger planets. Some of them may have been from smaller worlds, of course, in which case they would have had poor going in this red sand.

I walked until the soles of my feet were blistered and the pain in my bare feet was a red blaze before my eyes. I stumbled. I fell a number of times. The instinct for survival is a potent force in every man. It made me go on walking—until I saw the pinkness.

Out of my dreams had come a memory. Yes, once I had stood here mentally as I stood now, physically. I had seen that distant pinkness. I knew there was an urgent importance about the pinkness. There was something inside it I must have. Without fail. The sight of the pinkness was a spur to my spirits. I tried to run, but the sand was too hot underfoot for that. All I could take was one slow step after another, trying to forget the pain.

I walked and walked. For miles? I have no way of knowing. The pinkness was always at the same distance. No nearer. No farther away. Time became a lifetime of red sand and hot sun and my own parched nakedness. After a long period the sun was not so warm. I turned my head and saw it sinking.

And faintly in the sky I saw—a mighty band of glistening matter. I came to a full halt, gazing upward. A ring around this planet? Could it be Saturn? But no. Saturn was a world filled with methane and ammonia gases, or so Earth science told me. The sky beyond the haze of atmosphere here was naked to the eye, not filled with drifting mists of poisonous gases. Besides, the air was sweet to the lungs.

I turned back toward the pinkness.

It was easier now, the walking. The sands were not quite so hot, nor did my feet pain me so much. It seemed to me also that the pinkness was drawing closer. My strength was returning with the coolness of dusk, so that I walked on with renewed confidence.

Dusk was gone and night was a bright silver radiance over this entire desert when I came at last to the pinkness. From that glittering band of matter that turned slowly about the planet came reflected sunlight in a shower of subdued brightness. The red desert sands looked dark, black. Ominous. They went everywhere except into the pinkness.

Inside the pinkness was a shifting mist of rose and pale white and brightly shining silver that hid everything except glimpses of a black marble floor, highly polished, making a perfect circle perhaps two hundred feet in diameter. I came close to the edges of the flagging, finding a transparent wall before me shot with tiny red flames that gave to that wall a pinkish hue. The wall curved when it was twenty feet high, bending back upon itself to form a graceful dome.

I put my palms on the wall and pushed.

The transparent material was hard as glass. It did not yield. I walked around the wall, all around it, back to where I had started. There was no door to the thing, nor any window or other means of entrance I could see.

I tried to penetrate the shifting pink mists with my eyes, pressing my face as close as I could to the wall and straining my sight. I even hammered on the transparency for admittance, believing that the mists within it hid the source of the voice.

The voice!

Odd how it had abandoned me, once it had brought me to this world. As if its task were done, now that I had been delivered. The voice knew what this pinkness was. Long ago it had told me that the pink mists held something very valuable to the voice creature. I must get that prize set within the mists and—bring it to the voice-being.

I leaned against the wall. I came close to laughing with hysteria, from frustration. My eyes searched the sands. Hunting with ludicrous hope for a weapon, for a—a something— to act as a lever and thrust me though the wall.

But how?

It was then I saw the blue men.

13

They were far away, about five of them, and mounted on some sort of four-legged beast like a horse. It was not quite a horse. I saw slender horns jutting from foreheads and hides streaked with dark bars but I was too far away to see details.

My back pressed against the wall.

The blue men wore fur kilts and capes, with broad leather belts about their middles each holding a longsword and something like a revolver. Fur hats with upturned flaps gave them a barbaric appearance, and under the darkness of the fur across their chests I caught sight of a round medallion. Small white horns projected from the temples of the blue men, giving them an oddly beast-like appearance.

The foremost rider had seen me. His right arm went up and instantly the horned horse was a streak of barred lightning racing across the sands. It came with the speed and silence of the wind, barely rippling across the sands, and its rider was uncoiling a long rope as it ran, shaking out the noose.

The rope came fast for me, like a ghostly presence high above the desert sands. It settled down about my shoulders and it tightened, squeezing as if it were a living boa constrictor. I sought to turn, was yanked sideways off my feet. I fell to my knees, hampered by my arms pinned to my sides.

I dug in my feet, lurched sideways, backward.

The rider was yelling and laughing, coming for me, leaping from his mount—it was a horned horse with black streaks all over it, something like a big zebra—and gathering up the slack in the rope with infinitely deft hands. Up this close I saw he was very handsome, in a lean, saturnine manner, with faintly slanted eyes. His pale blue skin bulged with muscle.

He shouted something to the others, who laughed, reining in their mounts and watching with wide grins. They expected some sport, their faces told me. And I was the one to furnish it.

Again I rammed bare heels into the sand and lunged backward.

14

I felt the cold wall behind my shoulders. No help there. And then—

The coldness was spreading, enveloping me, gathering me into itself and letting me through to the pale pink mists that sang as I fell in among them onto the hard black marble floor. The rope was still about my shoulders. It had yanked my attacker off his feet, head first toward the wall as I fell, so unexpected had my action been to the blue man.

He rammed into the wall, which did not open to him.

He fell to the sand and lay still.

CHAPTER TWO

THE PINK MISTS sang in bright triumphant peals, like distant bells heralding a victory. It chorused with a happiness so infectious that I found myself laughing with it, like a madman. Pink sound. Pink music. Pink laughter coming from my throat to join with it in a paean of delight at my escape from death. I think I really was a little mad at that moment.

Through the pale hard walls I could see the other blue men—there were only four of them now, since their fellow lay crumpled just outside the wall—leaning forward over the striped cruppers of their horned mounts, staring. Their eyes seemed to bulge with disbelief. They stood frozen like that, forming a barbaric tableau. The wind ruffled the fur on their caps above their horned foreheads, but this was their only movement for several seconds. Then one of them opened his mouth, crying out, I believe, though I could hear no sound but the pink pealing of the unseen bells.

All four riders whirled and galloped into the night.

I drew a deep breath, felt exultation surge into my veins.

Exultation and strength, as if the mists were a form of parasensory energy I could draw into my muscles and my flesh merely by standing in it. As that energy flooded me, I found the mists dissipating, dissolving. As each wisp faded out, the bells grew more faint until they were gone entirely.

Now I could see what the mists had hidden.

A long dark altar of bright black stone stood in the geometrical center of the marble floor. Resting on the blackness, in a tiny niche seemingly created just to hold it, was a metal ball. I walked across the floor and put out a hand, lifting the metal ball and holding it cradled in my palm.

Was this the prize for which I had been wrenched from Earth and put down possibly a hundred or a thousand light years from the planet of my birth? This little thing was no bigger than a large marble. It tingled when I held it, but other than that, there was nothing remarkable about it.

My hand closed on it.

Somehow I knew that the little globe was infinitely important.

I turned away from the altar toward the wall. The blue man still lay there, motionless. A dozen feet beyond him stood the horned horse, ears pricked forward, waiting patiently. I decided that riding would be infinitely better than walking on these sands.

Still holding the metal ball I walked straight ahead. The wall no longer held me. I stepped through it and onto the red sands. I knelt above the fallen blue man.

He was dead. Apparently the hard wall had struck his head at such an angle when he lurched forward that his neck had snapped. He wore clothes. I was naked. It would be a simple matter to put on his fur kilt and throw his fur mantle over my shoulders.

Now that I was outside the pink mists, I found the night was cold. My skin crawled with gooseflesh and my teeth chattered. I undid the big gold buckle unfastening his broad leather belt, and stripped off the fur kilt and undergarments.

In a moment I was dressed in fur and leather, with a

sword at my left side and some sort of handweapon at my right. Leather boots that reached to the middle of my calves protected my feet from the sand. I put the fur cap on my head and the round medallion the blue man had worn about his neck into the belt pouch.

In front of me the transparent wall and the black floor with its odd altar was shifting, shimmering in the rays of the mighty band encircling this planet. I held my breath, watching the wall evaporate before me and after the wall, the floor, turning into black smoke and blowing this way and that to the night winds that roamed the desert. In a few seconds it was gone. Only the metal ball in my hand remained to prove the pinkness had ever been.

I put the metal ball in a small leather pouch which was part of the swordbelt. Then I turned toward the horned horse.

It was wary of me, sidling away and tossing its head so that the silvery mane shook like a silk scarf. I had handled animals on Earth often enough to be familiar with their nature. An old Indian guide had taught me the way Indians broke their mounts in the old days. I talked soothingly, with my hand stretched out; after a time the beast quieted and let me stroke its nose and neck.

I swung into the saddle of black leather ornate with silver mountings, and found it snug to my rump and thighs. I lifted the reins.

One look I laid about me, seeing the red sands where the walled pink mists had been and the dead, naked body of the blue man. My mind filled with chaotic thoughts. What did I do now? I had the metal ball, I knew it was important to my voice-being—whatever and whoever he was—but how was I to get it to him?

I waited a little while in the moonlight with the wind stirring the sand about the forelocks of my mount, before I sighed and gave up all hope of hearing the voice. With a toe I nudged the horned beast to a canter.

I had no way of knowing where I might find water,

17

and water was becoming an obsession with me. My throat was parched. Only the coolness of the night revived me enough to keep going. Otherwise I might have fallen and when the hot sun rose, it would find me easy prey.

I did not know, but the beast did. All animals know where there is water, by some sense atrophied in man. I let the reins fall loose. Under my rump the animal maintained a steady pace.

I was too excited to sleep in the saddle. I let my eyes assess the great band of brightness high above that was as a moving mirror reflecting sunlight from the big red orb I had seen during the daytime of the planet. It filled a quarter of the sky as it rotated swiftly, throwing off dazzling coruscations of light and color, rousing awe in me who had never seen such a sight on Earth. It seemed to whisper a little, too, as though the parts which formed it banged together in sonorous clashings.

It lighted up the desert for unguessed distances, lending a pallid light to the scene that made the shadow of the horned beast and myself on the ground blacker than it would have been under normal conditions. Later I was to learn that this band is comprised of the fragments of three moons which had circled the planet—called Llarn by its inhabitants—and had collided in a long-ago time. Instead of falling onto the planet, those moon fragments had come together in an orbit about one hundred thousand miles out in space. For more than fifty thousdand years they had circled Llarn.

I rode on and on through its radiance.

Dawn was a redness on the horizon when I saw the ruins. At first they were no more than a dark mass of stone humping upward here and there so that I thought them hills. Indeed, there were hills beyond them into which the ruins merged, so that it was not until I was almost upon them and the red sun was higher in the sky that I could pick out rows of pillars and the bigger bulk of buildings.

Hope surged into me. Where there were buildings, there must be water. My heels kicked the horned horse to a run.

I still held the reins very lightly, knowing the beast would find water before my own imperfect senses could detect it.

I cantered through an avenue of fluted columns held at their cornices by a long stone lintel that was cracked with untold centuries of existence. Beyond this long portico lay the city proper, wide and mysterious, a massy bulk of aged rock and masonry that stretched on and on. At one time, unknown centuries ago, this had been a mighty metropolis.

Deep within the maze of streets and squares, the animal found a well. It halted, shaking its head impatiently, as if expecting me to do something. I swung from the saddle and walked to the well. Far down I could see the reflection of sunlight on water, but how was I to get at it? There was no well bucket, no rope, no steps carved into the inner stone for handgrips and toeholds.

Wait! The lariat the blue man had used to catch me, yesterday! I had coiled it, placed it among the other objects in the saddle roll behind the saddle cantle. I stepped to the animal, fumbled with straps, and lifted down the saddle blanket.

Searching among the objects held by that length of dark wool I found a metal pot with slim handles through which I threaded the rope. Leaning over the well wall, I dropped it into the water.

I let the horned horse finish the first two potfulls before I lifted its rim to my lips and drank my fill. The water was pure, cold, delicious. I drank slowly for my thirst was great, sipping a little at first, then allowing myself longer swallows.

The water acted on me as might food. I felt filled with renewed energy almost at once. I was hungry, but food could wait. Besides, reason told me that there might be food as well as a pot in which to cook it, inside the saddleroll. I came off a stone bench where I had been sitting to examine the contents more closely.

I found a narrow jar holding round brown lozenges of some sort. I tried to bite one and found it hard as rock. I tried to dissolve it in the juices of my mouth but it was just as unpalatable. I forgot the lozenges in my sudden interest in what appeared to be a clip holding cartridges of some bright red substance. I drew out the handweapon from its holster the better to examine it. Yes, here below its barrel, was the bottom of just such a magazine. I fumbled about until I found a hidden spring that released it into my hand.

The clip in the gun was filled with these same red objects. Bullets of some sort, I supposed them. I replaced the clip in the gun and tossed the other onto the saddleroll. Since I was to live here on this world, I decided it was only wisdom to learn how to use its weapons. From what I had seen of the blue men, existence might become a precarious thing unless I familiarized myself with the handgun.

I lifted it, took aim at a distant outcropping of stone jutting from a building wall. As I did so, I heard a low humming sound, off to the south.

I rose to my feet, staring.

A dark object was streaking low across the desert sands, straight for these ancient ruins. It was moving with the rapidity of thought and it was that speed through the air that made the humming noise. Was it alive? Sentient? Some new danger to be faced? I took a firmer grip on the handgun and waited.

Three—no, four similar black objects came into sight, moving just as fast. From one of the following objects a needle beam of red light streaked, barely missing the fleeing thing. Again the red beam appeared. And yet a third time.

The third shot made the thing wobble.

Now I had a better look at the flat black thing with the odd hump along its top. It was a flier of dark wood, motored by jet propulsion. And the hump on it was a living person.

The flier was dropping fast toward the ruins, the person on it fighting desperately with its controls. I ran forward a few steps. I never like odds in a fight. Four against one was too rich for my blood. Justice or injustice in this matter made no difference. I would help the pursued if I could.

I ran forward, shouting and waving an arm.

The flier saw me, veered toward me, the flat deck wobbling erratically. It lifted and fell at a crazy angle, yawing badly. It dropped between the fluted columns with one side toward the ground and the other uptilted to the sky. Now I could see that the person clinging desperately to its control levers was a girl.

I leaped from the shadows of a building as she slipped over the side, caught by straps that were tangled about her legs and an arm. Her four pursuers were coming in fast and low, scenting victory.

The jet flier banged into a column.

My sword was out and slashing desperately at the straps. The girl hung in them helplessly, swaying a little as the crippled flier sought to rise, to fly on. I had no more than a glimpse of golden skin and some jeweled ornaments before the last strap parted to the edge of my blade and she tumbled down into my arms.

As my arms went about her, I gazed into an exotically lovely face. Slightly slanted green eyes stared up at me in puzzlement as a heavy red mouth framed words I did not understand. Thick black hair, cut in bangs above a wide low forehead and hanging down to bared shoulders, was bound with a chain from which hung little silver bells. High cheekbones and a dimpled chin, firm and strong above a lovely throat, added to a beauty that set my heart to hammering.

She said something unintelligable, and let me hold her a moment while she drew a deep breath. Then she began hammering my shoulder with a fist, crying out words that I could not understand. I gathered from her expression that she thought I was a fool to stand here in the open where her pursuers could take pot shots at us with the red needle beams.

I lowered her so that her sandals touched the paving stones. Then she was whirling, running away from me into the shadows of the buildings. She was like a cat in her movements, lithe and graceful.

The needle beams came at our heels, spurring us to a faster pace.

Where two buildings made an overhang, she twisted into a recess and stood there panting, staring back the way we had come. For the first time she seemed to see the gun in my fist for she sighed and smiled faintly, pointing toward it, then back the way we had come.

She said some more words and after a time stamped her foot imperiously. I said, "I'm sorry. I just don't understand you."

Her eyes widened at my speech and she pushed away from the wall recess as if really seeing me for the first time. Her skin was a pale honey color and her hair a glossy black. My white skin—except where it had tanned in the sun back on Earth—puzzled her. Except for the dolthoin, a race of men living in the twin oceans of Llarn, no other people of her world had white skins. Since the hair of the dolthoin was white and mine was yellow, she knew I was no water dweller.

She pointed to my fur kilt and jabbered, to my gun and said something else. Finally she rolled her eyes and sighed and leaned back into the recess again, disconsolately. I must have been something of a moron, in her eyes.

Now that she was quiet I could hear other sounds. Voices of men calling to one another and the hissing rasp of a red needle beam fired at full power. I showed my teeth in a cold smile. This was the second time I had been hunted in the space of roughly thirty hours. The blue man was dead. I thought it was time I set about killing the four men who hunted the girl and me in these old ruins.

Motioning her to get back deeper into the recess shadows, I moved on to the next street, which opened into a great square. I was halfway across the square when I saw movement out of the corner of my eye. One of the four pursuers had found me. The next instant a red beam was hitting the ground at my feet and moving straight for me.

It is a peculiarity of warfare on Llarn that a man need

22

not aim a beamer to kill his quarry. Since the needle beams hold their tightness, a man can swing it down or up or around in any direction once he begins firing. Sooner or later he will score a hit. If his target waits to be shot, that is.

I did not wait. His first shot had just scorched the flagstones at my feet when I was off them, diving for shelter behind a big block of stone. As I leaped, my hand came up and I snapped one vivid red burst straight for my attacker. There was no more sound. When I peered around the big stone block, half of him lay on the flaggings; I never knew where the rest of him went. I had scored a direct hit on his head and shoulders.

Luck had smiled on me. The Llarnians carry ornaments with them—the medallion on a chain which I had taken from the blue men was such an ornament—that counteract the deadly efficiency of the red needle beams. These roundels perform somewhat the same service to their wearers as do lightning rods to houses on Earth. Their peculiar metal absorbs the awesome powers of the red rays as soon as they come within a foot of anyone wearing them. My own medallion was in my belt pouch but because of my fur mantle my antagonist could not see that. And so instead of firing at me, he yanked out his sword.

I was happy to meet him with cold steel. I am an excellent swordsman—I have practiced too many hours with the rapier, the epee and the sabre, back on Earth, to indulge in false modesty. I knew the satisfaction of warm confidence when my hand went about my hilt.

My hand has always fit naturally about the hilt of a sword. My old fencing master used to say I had the soul of a Bergerac. My head and my wrist learned the Italian *finta da filo* as easily as they did the simple parry and there was a sympathy between them that made the steel part of me.

As the grinning attacker hurled himself and his sword upon me, my own blade flashed, parried, thrust in the deadly *botta in tempo*. With a foot of steel standing out behind his

23

back the man died, eyes wide and glaring, filled with disbelief.

I turned as a third man raced out of an alleyway, attracted by the clanging steel. He shouted something at sight of his two companions sprawled on the flaggings of this ancient city and raced across the square. Far down another avenue I saw the fourth man speeding to join us.

To face one man with a sword is a simple matter, to face two is more serious, especially in an open space. I hunted space for my shoulders to rest against a building wall but the man behind me gave me no opportunity. I was forced to turn and meet his sword. He played a waiting game, giving his companion time to come up to us.

The more delicate maneuvers of the blade I had to forego when I faced two men. I wove a web with my thin blade, slashing, parrying almost by instinct. For the first time in my life, I did not think as I fought. I let the magic in my sword loose as I freed the animal instinct of my body. I fought to stay alive, and to stay alive I had to kill these men. No time now for riposte and remise, only for the point moving in and out in its deadly dance, eluding the blades that sought to hold it, darting into openings no wider than the breadth of a finger.

I drove them both before me, giving neither opponent a chance to disengage and get at my back; across the great square I drove them with my sword and where a little flower opened red petals to the red sun above it, I caught one man with my edge across his throat.

My blade moved effortlessly into a parry to forestall the thrust his companion aimed at me. This man I pushed back into the shadows of a building overhang before my steel went into him. He fell facedown and never moved.

In that instant I heard the pad of running feet and turned, my point up and menacing. Barely in time did I recognize the girl and drop my blade before she spitted herself on the steel. Eyes wide, she looked at the four dead men, then at me, in something like awe.

24

She spoke; I shook my head. I did not understand her language and told her so. She frowned as I talked, looking deep into my eyes. With a little sigh she shrugged her shoulders and smiled.

Her teeth bit into her lower lip thoughtfully. Then she brightened and touched herself with the tip of her forefinger. "Tuarra," she said.

"Alan," I told her. "Alan Morgan. From the planet Earth." How to convey that bit of information stumped me, so I pointed at the sky.

When I did that her face went white. Twice she swallowed before she could whisper, "Epheloin? Epheloin?" I thought she was going to faint. It couldn't be all that bad, I thought, this—Epheloin.

After a moment she asked, in a voice only slightly less filled with horror, "Khorl?" I decided I was no khorl either, so again I shook my head.

She was so lovely, with that thick black hair of hers coiled high on her shapely little skull, a strand of which had come loose and tickled her bare shoulder, that I knew I had to learn her language, if only to keep her talking. She had the most melodious voice I have ever heard. It was like spoken music.

I squatted down and touched my toe. "Toe," I told her. Then my knee, my arm, my lips. She watched me with a pretty frown drawing her thin brows together. Then she giggled and hunkered down beside me, touching her own toe, her knee, her arm. As she did she said words slowly, so I might understand their inflection.

This would take a long time, but I was in no hurry. Being with Tuarra was a kind of giddy delight to me. Her presence made the blood sing in my veins and when her faintly slanted eyes lingered on me as they did from time to time, challengingly and with a touch of flirtatiousness in their depths, I damn near laughed with pleasure.

We walked back to the well and the horned horse, which I learned from her was called a dral, and I brought up

25

water for her to drink. She kept looking at my saddle roll and then at me, inquiringly. With a laugh, throwing her hands up in the air as if to ask her gods what she would do with such a numbskull, she went and got the narrow jar that held the brown lozenges. Opening it, she placed a lozenge on her palm and took it to a pan of water, into which she dropped it.

I stared as the lozenge began to grow and grow. Within five minutes, when she put her fingers into the water, she brought out a two inch thick steak, juicy and heavy, ready for cooking. My eyes must have boggled a little for she laughed and said something tenderly.

On Earth, through a process called freeze-drying, food can be stored away almost indefinitely, losing its water content and much of its weight, but retaining its same size. Here, they had learned to reduce the size also, in some manner as yet unknown to me, so that a small jar could hold enough food for a month, for a hungry man.

Tuarra showed me where to find a plant called thoril, the branches of which were dry and fragrant, making excellent fuel. Never had I enjoyed a meal as much as I did that first one I ate with Tuarra in the ruins of ancient Paloranis sipping cold well-water between bites of steak. Since she was as anxious to teach me her language as I was to learn it, she interspersed her bites with words from her language. Savants have told me you must live with a language to learn it. I began to live with a hearty will.

When the steak was gone, Tuarra put her sandalled feet to the flame. Doubling up her legs and holding them with her clasped arms, she began to sing. I stared like a child at the clean features of her perfect face, memorizing the curve of the heavy lips, the faint slant of her green eyes, the wide forehead that showed her intelligence. She knew I watched her, the minx; she sang on as she stared up at the stars and occasionally her mouth would twitch with laughter. I suppose she knew I was heels over head in love with her before I did; most women know these things intuitively.

26

When her longlashed eyelids began to droop she turned to lift a blanket and wrap it about her, holding out one flap in invitation. I shook my head like a gentleman and folded it about her, bundling it up. Her eyes were thoughtful as they studied my features while she lay wrapped in the blanket beside the flames. I wished I could know what she was thinking but the few words I knew of her tongue prevented my doing much more than telling her that the steak was good or the fire was hot; not much help in a situation like this.

She was asleep within minutes so now I could feast my gaze on her face without embarrassment. Her skin was the color of pale gold, that delicate color into which some skins turn with suntanning. Later I would learn that this was the natural color of her people, the Vrann. My own white skin was akin to the flesh-tints of the dolthoin, a race of Llarn that dwelt forever in the bluish-green depths of its twin oceans.

Llarn is a planet much the size of Earth, a little smaller, actually, so that its gravity effect on my muscles was not as strong as that of Earth itself. It was one of eleven planets that revolved about the red star-sun which its people named Alfan. As near as I can make it out, this star is unknown to Earth, though near the star Canopus, being distant from it by a little more than three light years.

Though Llarn possesses twin oceans, joined by a narrow ribbon of water that stretched across the upper half of the planet for close to nine thousand miles, most of its surface is land. It is a very old planet, far older than any in the solar system. Its mountains have eroded into mere hills, for the most part, though a range runs north to northeast across half the length of this world.

I was to learn all this much later, of course; I call attention to it now because my thoughts were concerned with wheres and hows. I had come across unguessable gulfs of space, in answer to a voice, but since my feet had touched the red desert the voice had not come to me. I felt abandoned, lonesome, and might have sunk into a slough of self-pity except for the fact that Tuarra stirred, turning in her sleep, and lay facing me.

Staring down at her exquisite features, I could feel only elation. No matter who or what the voice was, or what its purpose in bringing me here, I had met Tuarra. I was content to be with her. Already she was in my heart; to keep her before my eyes would be my goal in life from now on.

I gazed down at her until the cold wind, stirring through the wide avenues of deserted Paloranis, reminded me that beauty alone is never enough to keep a man warm. I cursed my stupidity in not having slipped into the blanket folds with her when the invitation was offered me. I shivered. I moved close to the fire and tried to curl into a ball with my back to its flames.

It was no use. The nights grow cold on Llarn and while the great band of shattered moons afforded light, it did not warm the flesh as did the sun. Suddenly I remembered the flier in which Tuarra had come to me. There had been silks there, and even they would be better than nothing.

I stood up and walked away from the fire.

My path to the flier lay across the great square where I had fought the four men. As I came into the square, I saw that their bodies were gone—no, not quite gone, for there was something whitely gleaming in the moonlight where they had lain. I went closer and my skin crawled when I saw that only skeletons lay where short hours before dead men had been.

I put my hand on the beamer as I stared around me. What manner of beast had come here to pick clean their bones? I had neither seen nor heard a sign of any living thing other than myself in Paloranis.

Nothing stirred. There was no sound.

I walked on toward the edge of the city and the row of pillars where the flier had crashed. It lay on its side with its metal keel against two of the columns. I took this opportunity to study it more closely.

28

It was flat like a surfboard and about thirty feet long, with a curving bottom edged by a metal keel. A small motor—a miracle of precision nuclear engineering, I learned later—gave the flier the propulsive force of a dozen jet rockets. The little ship could travel as fast, theoretically, as a mach-limit; no living thing could live at such speeds, however, so their practical speed limit is about five hundred miles an hour. There are no walls on these fliers, only metal rails six inches from the deck to which the occupant straps himself, and a curved transparency that serves as a windshield.

A small panel held half a dozen instruments. By lying flat on the padded deck, strapped on, a rider could work those controls with his free hands. Where the red needle beam had slashed, the flier was torn and rent, and part of its gravitic motor had been shot away. Somewhere around this dead city were the fliers that had belonged to the men pursuing Tuarra. On those, the girl and I could go just about anywhere on Llarn.

Selecting the largest silks I could find, I wrapped them about me and walked back through the shadows of the city to the fire. Tossing a few more thoril branches on the coals, I lay down with my back to the flames. In a moment, I was asleep.

Toward morning I woke to the tug of hands on my arms. I tried to raise myself from the flaggings but found myself tied hand and foot.

A blue face glared down at me.

CHAPTER THREE

MY FIRST thought was for Tuarra. I turned my face to see the girl on her feet, shivering in the coldness of the dawn, rubbing her arms and speaking swiftly to the blue man standing over me. There was a hopelessness in the slope of her smooth shoulders that told me better than any words the trouble we were in. Something of loathing touched her face when she looked at our captors. Blue hands reached for me, yanked me to my feet.

I found myself facing the big blue man who had first stood over me and glared. He was a handsome man in a kilt of spotted fur and broad red belt from which hung two handguns and two swords. A thin fillet of gold about his head indicated his high rank above the gilded horns at his temples. Long black hair hung down to his shoulders where the strands were gathered together and twisted into what looked to be heavy gold nuggets.

As I was held upright before him, the man drew back his lips in a savage snarl and drove the back of his hand full against my mouth. Since my ankles were tied, I went over backward into what was left of our fire. One touch of those coals on my naked flesh sent me rolling sideways out of them, after a moment of agonizing pain.

I rolled into the ankles of the man who had hit me, driving his legs out from under him, sending him flying. Sharp exclamations of surprise rose up from the others. The blue man lay where I had felled him, oddly limp. Then I saw a trickle of blood at his temple where his head had hit the well-wall.

His followers ran to him, bent over him, probing his injury. One of them looked at me where I had risen to my knees and his lips drew back in a silent snarl. He made a motion with his hands and I was lifted bodily into the air and carried to a horned dral. My ankle thongs were cut; I was dumped unceremoniously onto its saddle, with my wrists still bound tightly behind my back.

Tuarra walked to another beast and mounted, urging her dral close to mine. There was fear in her eyes as she watched the unconscious blue man lifted and placed on a sort of stretcher between two drals. From his trappings, I assumed the man I had felled was an important one among the blue men. How important he was I would learn along the route of march, after Tuarra taught me her language.

As I was watching the other blue men mount up, Tuarra toed her dral close to me; reaching out, she caught the bridle of my animal and urged it to a canter beside her own. One of our captors glanced at her and grunted, then turned away. Evidently she was to be my companion on the ride ahead.

The blue men moved out of the ancient ruins and along an unmarked path across the red desert. They went in double file, with the stretcher carrying their unconscious chieftain in the rearguard. There were fifty or more blue men in the cortege. They rode easily, without obvious interest in their surroundings; apparently they were in home country here, with little to fear.

As we rode, Tuarra pointed a finger at the blue men. "Azunn," she said, and looked at me. I repeated the word dutifully and pointed in turn to our captors.

This was the beginning. All the long day she talked to me, pointing at various objects, at other times making me understand what she meant by gestures. It is not too difficult to learn a language when all you can speak is that language. Besides, I had an intense desire to be able to converse with this girl who cantered so close to me that her leg touched mine from time to time. Her closeness, her interest in teaching as well as my own in learning, made me a good pupil.

The language of Llarn is fluid, filled with soft vowels and few harsh consonants, so that it is a pleasure to hear and, once mastered, a joy to speak. I had no similar Earth speech on which to form a base. I was as an infant; I must learn to talk all over again. Yet Tuarra made my lessons a constant delight with her soft laughter, her gentle teasings at my hesitancy, her soft applause—which she registered by a purring sound deep in her throat—at my few successes.

We stopped for the night camp near a stretch of hardened ground, an oasis of sorts without shrubbery or vegetation of any kind, yet containing water below, which the Azunn

reached by sinking a pipe fitted with a boring device. All
Azunn expeditions carry a number of these drilling devices,
powered by a turn-screw handle; in a matter of minutes
they have clear water flowing from an outlet valve into
cooking pots and flasks. The water was sweet and cold, a
liquid happiness to the throat after a day of riding across
barren desert sands.

Tuarra was my maid and my teacher at the evening halt.
She roasted my steak and baked a fluffy sort of biscuit that
actually melted when held in the mouth. It had a honey
taste to it. She kept up her teaching all through the meal;
occasionally a curious blue man would come and stand over
us listening, make a laughing comment and walk away.

Tuarra paid no attention to the Azunn. It seemed to me
that she did not quite consider them her equals. I was to
discover that she was intensely proud, that her rank in her
home city of Kharthol was that of daganna, or princess,
since she was the daughter of Drakol Tu, dagan—overlord—
of Kharthol.

To augment her spoken instructions, she began after the
meal to scratch numbers and symbols in the hardpacked
dirt of our campsite. These she also assigned names to, with
little sighs of exasperation that she could not make clearer
to me the ideas which she had in mind. Infinity to an Earthman is represented by the figure eight lying on its side. The
Llarn conception of infinity is a wavy line. Idea, too, is a
word with which we had a little difficulty, as was the verb
to love.

Naturally, we did not cover all this ground the first night.
The Azunn were many miles from the heart of their homeland. This expedition was a stab into the more northerly
territory, desert lands which belonged to no one race on
Llarn, but that were looked upon as a badlands, where nothing grew except the dry thoril shrubs and few dwarf plants.
They were several days' ride from home.

My lessons went on, day after day, as my body toughened
to the hot red sun and grew used to the scorching heat that

32

rose from the red sands. As my muscles hardened to the feel of the dral between my thighs, I began to feel more at ease on this alien planet. Earth and its memories receded in my mind, became like a dream existence known long ago.

We were on the trail close to twenty days when we sighted a distant city. We had come to the edge of the desert and left it behind us, three marches ago; now we rode through a countryside of undulating hills covered with a coarse green grass and here and there sparse groves of trees. A cool wind blew across this ancient land and soothed skins burned dark by the desert sun.

Tuarra lifted her arm, pointing. "Azorra, the home city of the Azunn," she told me. "Here rules Morlan Az, the man you hit so hard he has not yet recovered consciousness."

There was pride in her voice, pride that made me flush with pleasure, though I hastened to point out that Morlan Az had cracked his skull on a well wall. She shrugged idly, as if to say that this was a mere formality; what mattered most was that I had done it.

"I'm surprised they're treating me so well. If Morlan Az is their dagan, I should think they'd have buried their swords in my hide for what I did to him."

Her faintly slanted eyes studied me. "It is a custom on Llarn among all its people that when a ruler has been harmed, he himself must set the punishment, if he lives." She made a wry face. "I do not like to think about your punishment, Alan Morgan. It will be a very painful one. Morlan Az is chieftain of all the Azunn. He is a cruel man, hard and overbearing. He had only one weakness, I am given to understand by traders who have come among the Azunn with their wares."

"And what might that be?" I asked.

I did not understand the word Tuarra spoke then, and apparently she found if difficult to convey any idea of its meaning to me. Even as she was trying to explain, the blue men increased the speed of their canter to a gallop, all except those guarding the stretcher on which Morlan Az lay in a

33

coma. They brought up the rear, moving slowly and sedately. If it had not been for the fact that Morlan Az lay unconscious, we would have made far better time to Azorra. Our fastest pace had been a slow trot and even that had proven too much for the injured man to stand. And so a week-long journey had been made into a march that had occupied close to a month.

The Azunn did not separate Tuarra and me, a fact for which I was grateful, as we neared the great gate of the city. There were high walls about the metropolis and people stood upon them, staring and pointing. A few scarves waved; an arm or two was uplifted and moved back and forth; otherwise our progress was awaited without excitement.

It was only when Tuarra came closer that a wave of sound went among the blue people staring over the battlements. They called her name and pointed, and many laughed in delight, as though she were a rare prize for the Azunn to take.

"Azorra is a very old city," Tuarra told me, riding with her chin high and staring straight ahead. "Some historians among my own people claim it is the oldest city on all Llarn, having been built more than a million years ago, when a great ocean rolled up to its very gates."

"Its occupants seem to know you," I pointed out.

She frowned at that, as if puzzled. Her pride did not quite stretch so far as to imagine that her face and figure was known to the crowds on the walls of Azorra. After a moment, she shook her head, admitting that she could not understand it.

Outside the ruins of Paloranis, this was the first Llarn city I had ever seen. It was built of colored stone, pink and red and brown in alternating slabs that blended together in a pleasing whole. The stone was so old it flaked and crumbled at times so that a fine dust lay upon the streets. Its avenues were wide, paved with stone of varying shades of grey, with some black streaks running through it. From the walls of the buildings projected solars—grass bubbles that formed viewing

34

screens for the people inside—which afforded glances into their interiors. These solars were crowded with staring men and women.

It was almost as though we were expected. Crowds lined the sides of the wide thoroughfares, silent for the most part, except for that buzz of excitement at first sight of Tuarra. I might also add that I attracted a good bit of notice myself. I was not a dolthos, that much was evident from the heavily tanned state of my skin, and my yellow hair. Every dolthos the people of Azorra had seen, and these were few and far between, had skin the color of a flat white and hair to match.

These dolthoin are sea people, dwelling in and about the deepest parts of the twin oceans. They live beneath the sea, they skim the surface of their water world in fleet boats driven by rockets. They want no truck with land people and slay every Azunn or golden skin who falls into their clutches.

And so the people stared, first at Tuarra, then at me, all the way to a great building of black marble that Tuarra told me was the palace of Moltan Az. We dismounted, then Tuarra and I were led into this great edifice, side by side, my wrists still manacled by heavy chains.

Through a long corridor set with painted pillars we were conducted into a vast audience hall and toward a massive golden throne on which a blue woman sat. She was in the full ripeness of maturity and her skin was a pastel shade— the women of the Azunn have not the darker skins of their men—that might have presented a pleasing sight to my eyes if I had not read the cold hate and bitter anger on her patrician features.

Golden ornaments contained her breasts. About her slim middle was a belt of heavy golden plates from which hung a thin kilt of red silk. Golden sandals, reaching up almost to her calves, completed her garb. The contrast of the gold and the red silk against her pale blue skin was exotic and barbaric in the extreme, an effect added to by her high coiffure in which golden balls were set here and there in thick black hair. The tiny horns projecting from her temples were heavily gilded.

These horns are tiny things, no bigger than the last joint of the forefinger, of white bone and not as ugly to the eye as they might sound. The Azunn often decorate them with bright paints. They are black for mourning, in red and white stripes on festive occasions. Gold is the symbol of royalty among the Azunn, which is why the horns of Morlan Az and his sister, Ulazza, were gilded.

Ulazza was a beautiful woman, for all her pale blue skin, and those golden horns were the touch that added most to her appearance as a barbarian. She was a devil woman, roundly curved and enchanting, despite her inner fury.

In that anger her right fist was taut and hard, beating upon the great golden arm of the throne with monotonous regularity. It was a form of relief for the tension in her, that made her sit upright and glare at us with her emotions clear to read.

"Tuarra of Kharthol," she said harshly, looking down at the girl to my left. "It was a good day for the Azunn when you were turned over to us."

Tuarra frowned. "Turned over?"

The woman smiled. "By the express orders of Gorlun Duv, overlord of Kharthol."

"My father, Drakol Tu, is dagan of Kharthol!"

The blue woman laughed musically. "You know better than that, daganna. The same coup that pulled your father off the throne and pushed Gorlun Duv onto it—will bring better times to my people."

I could feel Tuarra quivering beside me with curiosity and anger, but it was now my turn to confront this woman of the Azunn. She had been cold toward Tuarra with disdain and dislike. To me she was all hot rage and bitterness. If she could have had her way, I would have been thrown to the torture at once. She leaned forward, thin nostrils flaring to her deep breathing. Then she lashed out at me with words.

36

"Decadent child of aporad parents! Khor! Son of a thousand dolthoin! Decayed offspring of a mad ephelos!"

She went on like that for a while. I assume her insults grew more deadly, but I was unable to understand them, my knowledge of the Llarn tongue being still a little vague. I understood enough, however, to know that it would be her pleasure to superintend my dying if Morlan Az failed to recover at the hands of the Azunn surgeons, and that it would take a long time, possibly an entire tarn. The only thing that prevented her from throwing me on the floor and beginning right now was custom. Morlan Az himself must speak the punishment I was to face.

I stood and listened, marveling that such a beautiful woman could be so deadly. After a while she ran out of words and sat there, panting. Then she spoke crisply to an officer at her elbow.

"They are to be confined in the Hall of Dead Things," the woman snapped. "Neither is to be mistreated. The woman, because she is a State hostage, the man because I want him fit to endure the death my brother assigns for him." She stared hard at me, then added, "It had been reported that yours was the hand that killed my nephew, the son of my brother, before the domed dwelling of the pink mists."

I remembered the blue man who had roped me and come at me before I fell through the transparent walls that had held the pink mists. I told her it was not I who killed her nephew but that his death was a matter of his own doing.

"Had he not thrown a rope about me, he would be alive this day," I ended, and no sooner were the words past my lips than Ulazza was off the golden throne and striking my face with the flat of her palm.

She was a blue fury, I give her that; and she was strong, too, for her palm stung when it landed. She was panting heavily in her excess of rage. When she paused in her attack, I smiled down at her.

"You are safe from me because you are a woman, Ulazza," I told her. "Already the only two Azunn men who have

37

attacked me—your nephew and your brother—have paid the penalty for doing so."

It was sheer bravado. I heard gasps rise from the throats of the blue men and women crowding the throne room. Evidently few of their captives dared to defy the Azunn. Well, I was marked for a long death anyhow. What I said now would neither add to nor subtract from my ultimate end.

Ulazza opened her eyes wide at my words. I saw grudging respect deep in their black depths; respect and—something else to which I could not put a name. She went on looking at me as if her interest had been awakened in me as an individual, rather than as an instrument of vengeance.

"Where are you from?"

As I had done with Tuarra, I pointed upward. Ulazza shook her head and her penciled brows puckered. I tried to say, "I come from another world, far away from Llarn," but I am sure I made a mess of it.

She gestured with her hand.

Armed men came and took us out of the audience hall. Before the great wooden doors closed behind us, I turned and stared back at the massive golden throne. Ulazza still stood before it, looking after me. It was then that I felt my side pinched, viciously.

Tuarra flushed as she said, "Just because she likes you, don't think to find mercy in Ulazza, Alan Morgan. She is crueler even than her brother. She takes delight in the tortures she dreams up for captives taken in war. You will curse her name ten times ten thousand times before she lets you die, if Morlan Az allows her the privilege of acting as your executioner."

"I wasn't aware that she liked me."

Tuarra scowled darkly. Her full red lips pouted and her eyes seemed to catch fire. She drew herself to her full height and lashed out at me with her hand. She did not have quite the hitting power of the blue woman, but my ears rang with her blow even as she turned and stalked away, head held high.

One of my captors grinned. "This one has the rare ability to make all women mad at him, it seems. Well, rather him than me."

A hand pushed me forward. I followed Tuarra quietly.

The Hall of Dead Things was a museum, a magnificent structure not far from the palace. The blue people did their best to maintain it as it had been a thousand years before, when they had moved in off the grasslands of Llarn to become city dwellers. Originally, the Azunn had been nomads, living in tents and making their livelihood from the vast herds of beef animals they maintained. They sold meat and hides to the gold-skins, together with horns and hooves, accepting in exchange metal with which to make their weapons and loom-woven silks and brocades.

Now the blue people, though still savage, were emerging from their nomadic state to something approaching civilization. As a corollary of that desired culture, they sought to keep alive the knowledge which the ancient ones of Azorra had placed inside the Hall of Learning.

On the floors above the mezzanine, there were many small rooms. Tuarra and I were to be assigned one of these. Guards would be placed outside the building, front and rear, at the only doors giving entrance and exit from the Hall. Otherwise, we were free to roam the building where and when we would.

The mezzanine itself was part of the museum. As we paced through it, I found my gaze being drawn to the walls which were recessed to form dioramas and tri-dimensional scenes out of the forgotten past of Llarn. I caught glimpses of strange boats with triangular sails and high, curving prows, of painted oceans with towering mountains in the background. There were no mountains like that on Llarn today, I felt sure, and could only guess at the incalculable age of this world I was on. I gazed on scenes where men and women whose skins were like my own laughed and played at games and walked under three great moons.

There were no moons on Llarn now, only that great band of brilliant matter always circling the ancient planet. I made a mental note to ask Tuarra about this when she got around to acknowledging my existence again. At the moment she was too engrossed in haughtily tossing her head to speak to me.

She went into the room assigned to us and lay down on a pile of sleeping silks spread close to one wall. She put a forearm over her face and appeared to sleep. I was too excited, too filled with the spirit of my adventure to doze in the middle of the day.

"Why not walk through the Hall with me?" I asked her.

She made no reply, but I saw her lips stiffen.

"This is a marvelous opportunity for me to learn more about your world," I went on. Still there was no reaction. "I'm sorry if I offended you by turning back to look at Ulazza. After all, she's the first blue woman I've ever seen."

When she remained silent, I said gently. "I'll leave you alone then, for the spoiled little child you are." Ah, she quivered to that remark! The forearm came down and she half rose to an elbow. Her lips parted as if to speak, but she thought better of it. Instead she lay down, turning on her side so that her face was to the wall.

I sighed. She was so lovely and so small, so helpless, a captive to the barbaric might of the Azunn, that I wanted to hold her in my arms, comfortingly. Words of apology trembled on my tongue, but I did not speak them.

Instead I turned on my heel and went out in the dimly lighted corridor, closing the door gently behind me. The fact that I had the run of the building roused a faint glimmer of hope in my chest. Somehow, I had to escape from Azorra. How I could get away from the blue people was a question that seemed impossible of solution. I could not go on foot; the Azunn would soon overtake me on their fleet drals. I could steal a dral, I suppose, but search parties would follow its tracks and recapture me. And there were no fliers among the seven cities that comprised the world of the Azunn.

Nevertheless, I ascended to the rooftops of the Hall, finding them flat in many places, steeply ridged in others. I possessed a clear view of the city and the grasslands that lay in green richness on all sides of its high walls, but found no inspiration in them. Those oceans of grass, where once flowed the waves of a true ocean, were far too vast to be crossed with any hope of success except in a flier.

It was with a heavy heart that I turned back inside the building. I walked more slowly now, for I had no desire to sit back to back with an insulted Tuarra. I moved along corridors fitted out with display cases in which were the ancient costumes, on lifelike dummies, of the people who had lived long ago in Azorra. At one time Llarn must have been a colder world than it was now, for the men and women both wore bulkier garments, of fur and cloth. They were a handsome people, too. I was unable to read the dusty plaques attached to the cases, but the displays themselves were more or less explanatory.

I found a science room and studied the machines and engines which had powered the boats and aircraft of the Ancient Ones, the motors that had lighted and heated their cities and their homes. Some of these I found vaguely familiar, for they were constructed in fairly similar fashion to their Earth counterparts. Others I did not understand at all, for many operated on scientific principles of which I was totally ignorant.

I found paintings and splendid groups of statuary, and an exhibit that held the stuffed remains of what at one time must have been ferocious beasts. Felines with horns, horses with horns, birds with horns, I found in great abundance. All animal life, even the blue people, had horns growing from their skulls. It was the reason Tuarra did not consider them quite human.

In one corner I came upon a family of blue apes. Horns protruded from their foreheads as they did from those of the

41

Azunn and I began to wonder if the blue people had evolved from them. I had no way of knowing. When Tuarra was talking to me again, I would ask her.

One thing alone eluded me in the museum.

Usually—at least on Earth—there is always a wing or a section of a museum devoted to weaponry and armor, to swords and firearms. I found no such display, no matter how hard I looked. Knowing that I could not begin to think of escape until I possessed some means of defense and attack, I searched more carefully.

Here and there in my wanderings I discovered doors, some bolted and some open to the touch. These doors led into other wings of the vast building, in some of which I found models of early Llarn cities, steles and artifacts which related the story of the planet when it was young. Someday I would learn to read those carved surfaces, but at the moment I was infinitely more concerned about a weapons room.

I was positive that one existed. The people of Llarn were too warlike not to have a past that was studded with militarism. Somewhere in this great stone pile was a wing that held such weapons.

I wandered far and long. As I walked I noted that the rooms never grew any darker though their windows showed it to be dusk outside. Gradually it was borne in upon me that the metallic strips running about the base of the walls and the edges of the ceilings were emitting a blue glow. The glow was a gradual thing, attuned as it was to the band of brilliant matter eternally circling the planet, which fed the strips with a radioactive form of luminescence. As the day brightened, this radiance died out. As the day darkened, it grew in power so that there was no visible moment when the bands began their glow. Inside the museum, it seemed always to be daylight, even though the windows turned black with night.

Then I chanced upon a corridor I had not as yet been in. At its far end were two great double doors, strongly bolted.

The bolts looked as if they had been added long after the doors had been standing. To guard against some terror that lay behind them? To keep out a menace which had no other way of gaining admittance into the building? I had no way of knowing but I was too anxious to find the weapons wing to worry about new dangers.

I slid back the bolts with a creak of metal long unused. I yanked hard at one of the doors and it opened slowly. I stepped into a galleried room, almost as wide as it was long, and pulled the door shut behind me.

The glowing metal strips made this room as bright as the others. My heart lurched in delight. Along every wall were great wooden racks fronted by sliding glass panels. Behind these transparent doors were swords, polearms, spears, of every make and variety. My palm itched to open a case and lift out a sword and its scabbard, to hang it to the chains rivetted to my wide leather belt.

I merely paced along the walls, studying the weapons hanging in their racks. Finally, when I could resist the urge no longer, I opened a small case and drew out a long dagger with an ornate hilt and crosspiece. The braiding on the hilt crumbled to powder as my hand went around it, leaving only the thin metal tang. This metal was strong, unharmed by time, as I proved by rapping it hard on the marble floor. I thrust the dagger into my belt and moved on.

At the far end of the weapons chamber I came upon another door. It resisted my every effort to open it. Yet it had a lock of sorts and so, thrusting the tip of my dagger into it, I wriggled and rotated the point to such good effect that I heard a protesting creak and the lock slid back. My palm on the door thrust it open.

Ahead of me lay a staircase leading into blackness. The metal strips did not go into the museum cellars. Well, no matter. It was a simple matter to pry a small strip loose and carry it down into those dark subterranean depths.

I found myself in a maze of tunnels. Everywhere there

43

was dust that seemed to have been undisturbed since before the blue men had come to dwell in Azorra.

The metal strip I held gave off its weird blue glow, lighting the way ahead of me for more than fifty feet. There were jars here, laden with gray dust, heavy cases and trunks along the walls. I wondered what strange objects I might find were I to open the lid of one. I did not pause for idle curiosity, however. I was too concerned with finding my way through this underground labyrinth.

Hope was a strong flame in my chest, now.

If I could find a way out of these cellars into open country, beyond the walls of Azorra—it might be possible to escape. Our captors would not know we were gone until long after the event. Tuarra and I would be on foot, true, but we could still walk the five hundred ern between Azorra and the ruins of Paloranis. I put out of my mind the awful trek across those burning red sands. No need to think of them until we were safely out of this city.

There was a faint blue glow ahead of me.

My heart began pounding in my ribcase. Had I been walking in a fool's paradise? If there was a light up ahead, it meant human habitation. I wondered what kind of man would live this far below the metropolis, content with stale air and dust for his only companions. But I was forgetting. These metal strips that afforded light in Azorra were automatic things. They worked with the radiation they received from the band of minute moons that circled Llarn. They could have been operating silently and unseen for half a million years.

I thrust my own metal strip into my belt and drew my dagger. As well go armed into that chamber up ahead as blunder in unprotected. I walked on silent feet. I turned a corner.

An old man lay asleep on rotting rags.

He must be asleep, but he did not breathe; at least, his chest was motionless, nor did his nostrils quiver to undrawn breaths. He was naked except for a black and silver kilt and a weapons belt that carried nothing on it besides two black leather purses. I came closer and with my dagger poised to strike, put a hand on his chest beneath which his heart should be.

He was cold and still. Dead, then.

I breathed easier, wondering how many centuries might have passed since he had lain down to sleep. In this dry cellar air his corpse would remain unrotted until Llarn fell into its sun.

From the body I turned to look about the chamber. On the walls were scrawled odd words and stranger numerals. It was as if the man had spent all his days in calculating abstruse mathematical problems, then had lain down to die. I found a jar or two that held the remnants of what once might have been a liquid. All the jar contained now was a dark, sticky substance with a sweetish odor.

I was sniffing at the stuff when I heard a sound.

The dagger came into my hand as I whirled. The body had not moved. Ah! Again I heard the sound, coming from the tunnel up which I had walked. An Azunn search party, hunting for me? I stepped into the shadows cast by a recessed door and waited.

The sounds were coming faster now, as if someone or—something—were trotting more swiftly. My hand tightened on the bare metal of my dagger's tang.

I froze.

I was bent forward in a crouch, staring straight into the most hideous face I had ever seen. The face was that of a beast—a blind beast to judge by the white eyes that stared at me without moving. There was no iris, no pupil, only that cloudy opalescence. Two great fangs like tusks jutted from a thin mouth that gaped to show big white teeth. I have no comparison by which to measure it with Earth animals. It was a rodent of some sort, as big as a tiger, with a straight hairless tail and sharp talons thrusting from its mighty paws. Its head lifted as it sniffed me out.

Its mouth opened and a high-pitched wail of indescribable

45

malevolence almost shattered my eardrums. At the same moment, the thing charged.

Without the dagger I would have been a dead man almost instantly. I leaped sideways, striking at the paw that came ripping toward my chest even while the beast was in midair. Blade and paw met and the sharp metal of the dagger cut into the flesh of the animal. The rodent screamed in mixed pain and rage. It fell lightly, turned.

Long used only to the narrow tunnels in which it hunted its prey—what prey could there be in these labyrinthine ways for such a meat-eater as this?—the animal was slow in maneuvering. It had counted too heavily on that first piercing scream to paralyse its prey. When its paws failed to sink into living meat, it was baffled.

As it swung about I was moving sideways, dagger at the ready. The thing was fully a hundred pounds in weight and stood close to three feet at his shoulders. It was a mean antagonist, one which I would sooner have given a wide berth, but it was allowing me no choice.

The brute turned, but slowly. Again I danced to one side, knowing now it could not see but that its actions were governed solely by its keen ears. I saw those ears twitching, moving this way and that like antennae.

With a hand that made no sound I lifted one of the dark jars filled with a sticky substance. I tossed it across the room. Instantly as it crashed the beast whirled, its ears vibrating as it gathered muscles to leap.

I hurled myself onto it, stabbing deep behind the left foreleg. Three times I struck before the rodent humped its back and flung me from it. The thing was immensely strong, amazingly fast. I was flying through the air and seeing it whirling and leaping for me—huge pads outstretched, razor-sharp claws extended to rip—before I knew what was happening.

I thudded into the far wall with the wind knocked from my lungs. The brute dropped on top of me. My every muscle was strutted against the excruciating pain of disembowel-

46

ment; I had seen it lifting its hindquarters for the movement even as it flew through the air.

The momentum of its body drove me into the wall a second time. My head snapped back against solid stone and I was out only a few seconds. When I came to, I found myself smothering under the weight of the heavy rodent. It was dead—it must have died in midleap.

I thrust the loathsome thing from me and got to my feet. And the hair lifted on the nape of my neck.

The dead man was gone.

CHAPTER FOUR

TUARRA WAS eating when I returned to the room that had been assigned to us. She did not look at me, merely gesturing at a platter of sliced meat and something that looked like a red vegetable, together with a cup of dark liquid which was to be my evening meal.

When we had finished eating, I related what had happened to me in the tunnels below the museum. She did not deign to look at me but I could tell from the tilt of her head that she was interested. When I spoke of my fight with the rodent she drew in her breath.

"It was a sleeth," she breathed. "I did not think there were any more sleeths anywhere on Llarn. For a long time we Vrann have thought it to be an extinct animal, as the pterikal and the orlikon are extinct."

When I spoke of the dead man who had vanished, it was clear she did not believe me. "You were over-wrought. Excited. Your eyes played tricks on you. The dead do not walk away from their last resting place."

"Of course not. Therefore, he was not dead."

Her eyes grew very wide, suddenly. "He may have been a khorl!"

"What is a khorl? I've heard you use the term but I don't understand it."

She frowned prettily. "There were no khorls before The War. Afterward—khorls existed and azunn and huul, together with many other life forms Llarn had not known before."

"What war?" I prompted.

Tuarra gave me my first Llarn history lesson. It seems that many, many thousands of years ago there was only one race of people on the planet, the golden-skinned Vrann. Though they were all of one appearance, they had many great nations, Kharthol, Meradion, Loth, Pellavamar. A dispute between mighty Loth and Meradion drew in Kharthol and Pellavamar to preserve a balance of power. These were great civilizations, spread across the planet. Their weaponry was vast, terrifying.

The ruler of Loth, the almost legendary Ventrol Voor, ordered out his nuclear might. His war fleets filled the skies and the oceans, of which there were eight in those days. With him fought Meradion. Kharthol and Pallavamar went to meet them.

The result was—The War.

All Llarn had no other term for that year and a half of atomic destruction. When it was over, radioactive winds swept a dead world. All four great nations, all their cities, were graveyards.

Here and there, pockets of the golden-skinned ones still lived on. There were some who were trapped on islands in the sea, and since there was no food to be had on the land, they went into the waters of the oceans and there they lived to become the white-skinned dolthoin. Others were caught on the barren highlands, and these ate the radioactive vegetables and animals that still existed. Though many of them died, some lived to develop an immunity to the radioactive winds and food, and these became the aporads.

Her own people, the Vrann, had built underground hide-outs, stocked with foodstuffs. The living quarters were cramped, but the Vrann managed. After a great time the radioactivity died down and the little groups of the golden skins emerged from their shelters to find their old world swept away.

The Vrann learned that the radioactivity had caused mutations among the animals, which resulted in the Azunn people evolving swiftly from the blue apes to humanity in the arboreal jungles in the southlands which had been their home for uncounted ages. There were other mutated peoples living on Llarn now, all in a state of semi-savagery. It was like seeing their distant, prehistoric past come to life.

There were three known races on Llarn, now. There were the golden skins, the groups to which Tuarra belonged, called the Vrann; there were the blue men, the Azunn, risen from savagery to a barbaric civilization in the long centuries after The War; and the dolthoin. These last were the water dwellers, whose domain was in the twin oceans and the long channel that linked them together. In the ethnic groups unknown to Tuarra were the mythical aporads and the fabled huul.

"What about the khorls?" I asked.

"I'm coming to that. Here and there among the golden ones, individuals mutated, too. Among these are khorls, descendants of those early mutations. The khorls are outcasts—feared by all. They have strange powers, magical abilities that no one but other khorls can understand.

"There are the epheloin, too. As some of the animals evolved a billion years in a thousand, so too a few of the golden people also evolved into what we are to become—eventually. The epheloin are not men but beyond-men. Energy beings, perhaps. We are not sure. The epheloin pay us no heed, as we do not heed the insects underfoot. They are—something else. Not-men."

She cocked her head at me and smiled. "Now you know why we call it The War. It altered our planet and its people

49

completely. We still live in the cities of the Vrann, as their descendants. We have picked up the threads of their culture, tried to impose that culture on the rest of Llarn. It has not been a thankful task."

She let her shoulders droop in dejection. Apparently she was considering the fate in store for her at the hands of the Azunn. When I mentioned it to her, she sighed.

"I have been thinking about that. From what we have seen and heard here in Azorra, I am beginning to believe that the traitor Gorlun Duv entered into some sort of agreement with Morlan Az. Morlan Az was to hold my father and me as his captives, in exchange for certain advantages which Gorlun Duv would put in his way."

I frowned. "Back on Earth, there'd be only one reason for Gorlun Duv wanting you kept alive. If he married you, he would ensure a legal acknowledgment of his right to the throne of Kharthol."

"Yes," she nodded, "it's what I am afraid of. Gorlun Duv keeps my father alive as a hold over me. I might refuse to wed him to save my own life, but he knows I would never refuse him if by doing so I should condemn my father to death."

I glanced at her. "The longer you stay out of the clutches of Gorlun Duv then—the better are your chances for eventual safety."

She murmured heavily, "Gorlun Duv commands the might of Kharthol. Its armies call him lord. And the army of Kharthol rules the state."

I grunted. Earth had had its own assortment of military dictators in the past half century. Llarn was not free from the same social disease, it seemed. I sat thinking. After a while I roused to tell her about my hopes of escape.

"If we can find a path through the tunnels below the city, we might be able to go out under its walls. By the time they discovered we were gone—we could be many miles away."

I thought to cheer her but she seemed more sorrowful

than ever though she did manage a wan smile. "I thank you, Alan, for caring about what happens to me. But it is no use. There is no escape from the Azunn. One would need a flier to flee from them and the Azunn keep no fliers."

"There are four fliers in Paloranis," I pointed out.

"Paloranis lies half a thousand ern to the northeast of Azorra. Four days' ride on fast drals. It took us three weeks but that was because we marched slowly so as not to injure Morlan Az. On foot it would take us a few days more than that to get there. I am afraid it's no use."

"I'd rather die trying to escape than perish here in Azorra." I hesitated then added, "I don't blame you for wanting to stay. You will be queen in Kharthol in a little while. I—"

She went white at my words. Regally she stood up, staring down at me. Her face was a mixture of emotions, anger and doubt, revulsion and—something to which I could not give a name. Then she bent and picked up her sleeping silks and stalked haughtily to the furthest corner of the room where she lay down and wrapped herself up. Her back was a rigid line of anger.

At least she had not slapped me.

I sat for hours with my elbows on my knees, staring at the floor. The force behind the voice that had brought me to Llarn had been silent for so long I had almost forgotten its existence. What was its purpose in lifting me off Earth, for teleporting me to Llarn? What mission must I accomplish for it?

I drew the metal ball out of my belt pouch and turned it over and over. Vaguely I understood that the metal ball was of the utmost importance to the voice. I must bring the ball to the voice, I assumed. But if the voice did not reveal itself, how was I to do it? Moreover, as a prisoner of the Azunn, I was scarcely at liberty to do so.

I would not count on the voice getting me free. For all I knew, it might be dead. No, I would do better to rely on my own strength to effect that escape.

The tunnels were my sole hope.

51

I told myself that in the morning, with or without Tuarra, I would go down into those tunnels again and make my try at freedom. From the museum weapons rooms I would take a sword and a firearm—if there were any firearms in good working order—and begin my hunt through the labyrinthine cellars. Thus resolved, I lay back on my sleeping silks.

How long I slept I do not know.

But suddenly—

My eyes were open and I was rising to my feet, my hand going instinctively to the dagger in my belt. The door to our sleeping chamber was brightly glowing. Through its brilliant redness I could see the outline of a body. I crouched, waiting, dagger ready to strike.

"Who are you?" asked the figure in the redness.

"My name is Alan Morgan."

"No, no—I mean—who or what are you? You are no Llarnian. I have sought to bring you to me and—I cannot. I could do that with any living thing on this planet. What protects you?"

There was movement to my left, from the dark corner where Tuarra had been sleeping. She was awake and listening, breathing softly. Out of the corner of my eye I could see her propped on a golden elbow, leaning forward, staring.

"I come from a distant planet. How distant I do not know. I was teleported here by an unknown agency." I had decided that the voice and the metal ball were to be my secrets.

"That explains it, then," the being said. Its head turned in the redness and now it looked at Tuarra. "You are with the daganna of Kharthol. Why?"

There was an imperious note in the voice of this thing that annoyed me. "Who are you? What are you that you can walk around inside doors that glow red-hot?" I asked.

"The redness is not heat. It is my magic."

"A khorl," whispered Tuarra.

A chuckle was her answer.

The figure in the redness seemed lost in thought. When it next spoke, I caught an undertone of suppressed excitement. "You are captives of the Azunn. You will want to escape. I will help you do so."

"Why?" I growled.

"Out of pure self-interest. There is something I want, man of another world. Something which you can get for me. Agree to do this and I will agree in turn to save you and the princess of Kharthol from Azunn torture."

I turned to look at Tuarra. She was ashen, shaking in fright. "What about it?" I asked her bluntly. "Do you want to stay or will you go with me?" I had already decided that khorl or no khorl, if this thing could get me out of the clutches of the blue men, I would do whatever it wanted.

She touched her lips with a tonguetip. She was a very frightened girl; she had quite forgotten that she was a dag-anna. There was hope in her slant eyes and hopelessness in the droop of her red mouth. To go meant an unknown fate, to stay meant an awful one. She touched me an instant with her glance.

My heart banged in my ribs at what her stare told me. She was putting herself completely in my power. I had protected her from the four men despatched by Gorlun Duv after her; I would continue to protect her. She trusted me.

"You make the decision," she said softly.

I nodded, and turned back to the glowing door. "We will do what you want. I will get whatever it is you desire— in exchange for our freedom." As suspicion rose in me, I added, "When you have what you want, I will be free to go where and when I will, with the princess Tuarra?"

The figure nodded, "It is so agreed."

"What are we to do?"

"Go to the chamber where you killed the sleeth. I will be waiting there for you. Together, we three will leave Azorra this night and be in Krondys."

Tuarra was beside me, her warm little hand clutching my wrist. "Do not trust him, Alan. A khorl has no faith, no conscience. What a khorl wishes is its only law."

"Can you think of a better way out of Azorra?"

She shook her head until her black hair flew. Abruptly she had lost her haughtiness; she was a woman, no longer royalty. The khorl and I were her only hope. She feared the khorl with an ancient terror; me she tolerated, might even be friendly with me as long as I served her.

Oddly enough, I found I did not care. Just to be with her, to be able to see her patrician profile and her exotically beautiful face, was reward enough. I would do all I could for Tuarra of Kharthol, raise her to the throne itself if necessary.

"Tell me more about these khorls," I asked.

She shuddered."Long, long ago, right after the war, the first khorl was found to exist. It could make things happen—shape matter into whatever form it wanted, change people into beast-things—all with a wave of a hand and a few words. Never before did we of Llarn believe in magic. Now we knew that it existed and that the khorls were its masters.

"Since then they have been hunted down and exterminated. They rarely reveal themselves to anyone, now. They hide in dark cellars such as the one you found below the museum, in very ancient ruins, in caves in what few high hills remain."

"Is there any way to know one except by the magic he practices?"

"No, unfortunately. A khorl looks just like anyone else." Her green eyes slid sideways at me. "I thought you were a khorl at first. I am not—certain about you yet. Perhaps the khorl in the cellars—the one man you said was dead—is a good friend of yours."

I did not bother to reply to her. Instead I told her of the weapons rooms in the lost wing of the Azorran museum. She took heart at that, for I have learned that weapons are as the air itself to a Llarnian. Give a Llarnian a sword and he will defeat the world; such is their philosophy. The War took away their old culture and left them this savage battle for existence as an inheritance. Their ancestors had fought to stay alive in a radioactive atmosphere. They fought to keep that life which was their heritage, against all enemies.

As we slipped out of the cubicle and along the dimly lighted corridor toward the lower levels, Tuarra assured me that she could use a grawn, which was her word for revolver. The Llarnian handgun is powered by a manufactured compound which emits a faint electromagnetic wave. By channeling this wave in a straight line, by activating it with a tug on the trigger, it fires a beam of irresistible power which will blow a hole in as much as a foot of steel. It will kill a man instantly.

Tuarra showed me the medallion which hung about her neck on a thin metal chain. I recognized it as the same type of roundel worn by the four men of Gorlun Duv whom I had slain in Paloranis. At her insistence, I lifted the medallion—which she named a kranth and which I had taken from the blue man outside the dome of the pink mists— out of my belt pouch. Tuarra opened the chain and hung it about my throat.

To do so, she must come close to me. There was a fragrance to her golden flesh that was more rare than the spices of Araby in my nostrils. She was more lovely than any woman I had ever known. As her bare arms lifted to drape the chain, it was as if she embraced me. I put my arms about her and drew her close.

She may have been surprised by my action. At any rate, she offered no resistance when I bent my head and kissed her. Her lips were like heated satin under mine. In that instant while she clung to me, quivering a little, I knew I loved Tuarra of Kharthol more than I did my own life.

She drew away, frowning as if troubled. She did not lift her eyes to mine, nor did she say a word. For such a proud woman as the daganna of Kharthol had shown herself to be, I expected another slap, at the least.

"I love you," I told her in my own tongue.

She still did not look at me. Only her hand came up, gesturing me to walk ahead, to lead the way to the weapons

55

room. I shrugged my shoulders. The dusty museum of Azorra was no place to pledge my love.

Growling under my breath, I pushed past her. I walked swiftly but I could hear her sandals padding behind me. I may have offended her, but Tuarra had no intention of being left behind.

When we came at last to the bolted door of the weapons chamber I lifted out my dagger and picked the lock a second time. She seemed surprised by the ease with which I managed it. She muttered something under her breath which did not sound complimentary; the word I caught was corlth. I racked my brain for its meaning and the closest I could come was thief.

Later I was to discover that the guild of thieves on Llarn was very powerful. Life had become so hard over the centuries since The War that many people had existed only by taking what was not theirs. During the years of emergence from the shelters, theft had become a way of life for many.

Corlth, I was to discover, meant a master thief. Among other thieves, it was the highest compliment that could be paid a man. At the time I was indignant. Tuarra had her ways of striking back for fancied slights, I was to discover.

I brought her into the weapons chamber and watched awe touch her features. "Never have I seen such a room," she breathed. "There was nothing left of ancient Kharthol that housed such swords, such grawns. These are the original weapons of the Old Ones."

She ran to display cases, searching one after the other. Finally she reached in and drew out two handguns. One she handed me, explaining its mechanism. The other she kept in her right hand. I let Tuarra select a sword for me and a dagger for herself. We hung scabbards in the belt-chains provided for them, which had been empty since our capture.

Armed, she announced that she was ready to face the khorl. She looked so grimly determined that I grinned. She smiled ruefully. "You do not know how we of the Vrann dread the khorls. Since we were children, such a fear has been dinned into us. I never in my wildest nightmares imagined that I would see a khorl, though—much less depend on it for freedom."

A Llarn bogey man, I thought, and took her elbow.

Side by side we left the weapons chamber, moving past the doorway through which we could see the cellars stretching dark and mysterious. In my hand I held a strip of blue metal that glowed more brightly as we entered the cellar tunnels. Tuarra was close to me; I felt her warm little hand sliding down my forearm to clasp my free hand. The trust with which her fingers clasped my own gave me a speechless pleasure as is the way with lovers.

We encountered no sleeths, nothing but dusty tunnels as I found my way once more into the underground chamber that was the home of the old man. He stood waiting for us in one of three green circles he had marked out on the floor with paint.

"Stand you in each of the other circles," he told us.

As I hesitated, he smiled reassuringly. "They are only to act as catalysts to my magic. It will make the transportation—easier."

As my hand touched Tuarra to urge her forward, I felt her shuddering. Her skin was very cold. One glance she threw at me, her green eyes beseeching me not to fail her in this most terrifying moment of her life. I nodded to comfort her and took my own place in a circle.

The old man—his name, he told us, was Kav Mork—lifted his hands and spread his fingers wide. Their tips were smeared with some of the ointments that had been in the jars. The concoction gave off a too-sweet smell.

I had little time to notice smells, though.

Tuarra cried out and the hair rose on the nape of my neck. The room about us was fading from sight. Thin white mists surrounded us, through which I could see Kav Mork and Tuarra. Then they too were gone and I floated bodiless in utter cold.

CHAPTER FIVE

A REDNESS SHOT with black streaks was all about me.

A sense of otherness, of cold that was not cold but terrible warmth, and a dizziness in which only the brain was still alive held me in thrall. Faintly, as at a far distance, I felt the touch of frightened fingers and heard the whimper of a woman. There was no reality except for those fingers and the sound and the sight of colors running in a wild potpourrie of red and black.

Then the world turned solid underfoot.

I stood with Tuarra and the khorl in a small room the walls of which were black with age. Overhead were thick wooden beams and a brass lamp swaying, dimly lit. The lamp threw dark shadows on the face of Kav Mork, turned his twisted smile into something vile.

Tuarra turned, crying out, and hurled herself against me. For once, the pride of this daughter of Kharthol had broken under stress. She shivered against me while I soothed her with a hand on her thick black hair and whispered words meant only for her ears. The khorl watched with unwinking black eyes.

"It is time to leave," he said at last, turning away. I felt Tuarra cling to my forearm until her nails dug in. At the strained oaken door, Kav Mork looked back impatiently, saying, "It is time to pay your fee, to fetch me—that which I want."

As Tuarra shuddered, I realized we had no other choice. I had made a promise; I intended to keep it. When I had done what Kav Mork wanted done, we would be free to leave. I told Tuarra as much as I guided her toward the door with an arm about her middle.

"I don't trust him," she protested in a vehement whisper. " 'Never trust a khorl, if you love life' is an old saying in Kharthol."

"Nevertheless, I promised," I answered her.

We went into the corridor of what was apparently the underground remains of an ancient cellar. As we followed Kav Mork's swaying black robe, Tuarra informed me that khorls always lived in cellars—not that they dreaded the sunlight of the surface but here, far underground, few people ever ventured. The inhabitants of the city streets figured that if they left the khorls in peace, they themselves would remain unharmed.

Along the stone floor of the corridor and past twisting tunnels and up a ramp we walked. Once I heard the slap of water against a timber piling. Tuarra seemed surprised when I mentioned it to her, and her pretty brows wrinkled in thought.

"A city beside the sea of Markool? It can only be Krondys. To distant Kharthol, Krondys seems in another world."

We came out into the red glow of a rising sun. The journey from Azorra to Krondys had not taken very long; it had been close to dawn in the city of the Azunn when we teleported here. Kav Mork waited for us, standing dark and ominous before the door he held open with one hand.

The street was cobbled underfoot as he brought us between massive buildings that seemed old as the planet itself. Before The War, Krondys had been a great market center for the goods of its world. Mighty warehouses had held the silken stuffs of Tay, the precious stones and carved metalware of Skolthoon, the rare herbs and spices of the Seven Islands of Opalorn. Krondys still brooded down on the ancient streets which had known the footfalls of the ancient heroes, Foll and Dikerbann. The wind was fresh, laden with the scent of salt.

There were few travelers on the avenues at this early hour.

A cart rattled on its wheels a block away and from some-where up above, a woman called a name. Three men came out of a tavern, yawning and stretching their arms. They glanced at the khorl and hurriedly averted their eyes, turn-ing back into the wine shop from which they had just come, crowding upon each other's heels. Evidently khorls were as feared in Krondys as they were in Kharthol.

"Teleportation?" I asked Kav Mork suddenly.

He glanced at me from under shaggy brows, eyes bright and luminous. "Yes, teleportation. These fools think it's magic." His hand indicated the buildings all around us. "The radioactivity of The War altered our brains as it altered the bodies of the others. We khorls were able to develop a telekinetic energy with our brain waves. We can do—many things—with that energy. Things that seem monstrous to the uninitiated."

His smile was twisted. "What a man does not under-stand, he fears. So are we feared, on Llarn. We play up to this sense of dread, pretending it is magic that gives us our powers."

"The circle on the floor, back in Azorra, and the oint-ment on your fingers," I murmured. "All of them are stage props?"

"Something of the sort." His head nodded. "Do not imag-ine that we need them, however. They are a gloss like a veil we draw in front of ourselves, to add to the fear in which we are held. We are shunned, and that is a good thing, since it gives us more freedom."

As Kav Mork and I conversed, we came to the end of the cobblestoned street. Before us lay a great quay, the stone walls of which went down into a wide expanse of water. As far as the eye could look, there was a surging, rippling sea. A dozen vessels were moored to wooden pilings, to pre-vent them from bumping their wales.

Kav Mork pointed to a slim ship with a lateen sail bellying in the breeze. "Mine," he announced, and crossed the quay-stones toward it.

Tuarra hung back, shaking her head. "Don't go with him. He is taking us to our deaths."

"He could have killed us back in Azorra if he wanted us dead," I pointed out. "Besides, even his magic is useless against a quick dagger thrust."

She was unconvinced by my logic but she walked beside me, letting me balance her with a hand as she stepped down onto the moldboard and then to the narrow deck. Kav Mork was at the mast, checking the clew lines. Aft of us, there was a black wheel that served as a helm. Forward, a little cabin, also of that same dark wood, showed empty in the radiance of a hanging lantern.

There was a sombre quality to the black ship that raised the hair at the nape of my neck. It was something out of nightmare, all black wood and red metalware, with a striped red and black sail quivering above our heads almost as if alive and eager to be off and running.

Tuarra was quiet, as though pride had conquered her fear. Her eyes went with mine all over the ship, watching Kav Mork cross to the helm, unfasten the leather thong that held it, and swing it lazily. Instantly, the ship began to move backward, away from the quay.

There was no breeze stirring, nor was there the sound of a motor. Just the water gurgling below and the sense of movement transmitting itself through the deck planks.

And then, as the ship swung about—

I felt the sea breeze, strong and steady. It came up suddenly from the south over the rooftops of the city and it blew outward across the waves. The black ship lurched, quivering as it gathered speed. Aft, its wake made foaming bubbles. Swiftly the ship flew, swiftly it cleaved the waves while the following wind never diminished but, if anything, increased in intensity.

"You saw," Tuarra whispered. "You saw how he summoned up the wind and made it obey him."

I tried to tell her something of telekinetic energy, as much as I understood it, but failed miserably. Her wide green eyes

61

searched my face as I talked and in them I read pity and a great tenderness. Evidently she thought Kav Mork had mesmerized me in some manner on our walk to the quay.

The day went on toward evening. The sky clouded over, grew darker as night overtook us. Kav Mork stood like a statue at the wheel, as he had stood unmoving all during the long daylight hours.

When the lantern in the cabin was the only illumination anywhere on the ship, and the night darkness pressed in about us like some alien menace, Kav Mork tied the helm with a leather thong and made his way forward.

"There is food in the cabin locker," he muttered.

I realized for the first time that I was shivering. The salt wind had been growing colder with every passing hour, losing the warmth of the tropic region in which we had started, gathering within it the chill of the northern climes.

The cabin was warm. Red coals glowed in an iron brazier and the single lantern was aided by three others. Tuarra pointed out to me in an aside that Kav Mork had not moved from the wheel until just now, yet there was a fire in the brazier and blazing candles in the hanging lanterns. When had he done it? I did not know; it was enough for me to walk to the brazier and extend my hands over it. Instantly Tuarra was beside me.

"Magic," she breathed. "I told you the khorls were magicians."

"Magic or mind over matter," I grinned, "the fire is still warm. So enjoy it."

Her glance told me she did not expect me to understand these mysteries, being no true Llarnian, but the least I could do was realize the seriousness of the situation. I tapped the hilt of my longsword for an answer. Underfoot the ship plowed through the Markoolian Sea, shuddering as might a living thing at its cold waters, and I wondered vaguely in my mind if the ship might be alive, at that.

Tuarra was close to my side and pressing closer. I had a sword at my hip and the devil in my heart. A dozen Kav

62

Morks would not have frightened me at such a moment. I ran my hand up and down Tuarra's bare arm. She turned her head and stared at me. Slowly her lips curved into a smile, and I realized quite suddenly that because of my action and what she saw in my eyes, she was no longer afraid.

Kav Mork passed two wooden platters at us, each of which was heaped high with steaming meat and freshly baked bread. We ate, Tuarra and I, pressed together so that our hips and shoulders touched, close by the iron brazier and its red, red coals.

When we were done, the khorl leaned forward and filled two leather jacks with a pale red liquid, from a leather pitcher. Gravely he handed them to us.

"It is time to speak of what I want you to get for me on the isle of Inislan," he said softly. His eyes were half closed, and there was an ashen pallor to his cheeks.

"Long ago, before The War," he began, "the isle of Inislan was the holy place of a sect of demon worshippers. They built a citadel there of which little remains but two walls and a fallen roof. A flier filled with nuclear weapons crashed close by and—but there's no need to tell you about that.

"It is sufficient for you to know that the citadel is now the home of a form of animal life against which my own powers are useless. It hasn't the intelligence to respond to my mental superiority. It takes a brave man—with a weapon in his hand like that longsword you hold—to overcome it."

I had the feeling he was laughing at me in some manner I could not understand, but his face was sober and his eyes blank and staring. "This creature has lived as long as I, perhaps longer. It has immortality, of a sort. It can be killed but—few men can get close enough to do it. I call it a salorth."

"And when I kill the salorth?"

His hand made a casual gesture. "You are free to go, both

of you. I will put you down in any port where the sea of Markool touches."

"I don't mean that. What are you after?"

For the first time, he smiled. "A treasure. Oh, not gold, not jewels. Something far more precious, for which there is no duplicate anywhere on Llarn"

His compelling eyes turned from me to Tuarra, then back again. In their dark depths I saw unhuman glee. His tongue touched his thin lips.

"A treasure that shall give me undreamed of powers. Yes, and wealth, too—as men measure wealth. I have grown tired of my life as a khorl. I—"

It was Tuarra who lashed out at him, chin up and eyes feverishly bright. "The world is no place for a khorl. Everywhere you go, you inspire terror. Children would run from you. Women would faint at sight of you. Men—"

His hand went up to stop her flow of words. His dark eyes blazed as though with distant fires in their depths. I choked back a curse, half rising to my feet. For his face was changing, altering before our very eyes.

No longer was his skin pale and withered as old parchment. It fleshed itself, grew firm and brown. The contours of his body were growing, too, filling out the robe. Slowly he came to his feet. Hair was growing on his head. Youth was in the lines of his face, youth and strength and a kind of male beauty.

"Fools, the two of you! Do you think I am hindered by the outer shell which I show the world? From the very atoms and the molecules that shape my body I can make myself look like—this!"

The robe fell. In a short kilt and jerkin, Kav Mork was a twenty year old youth, his body brown and heavy with muscle, no longer the scrawny ancient. His eyes touched Tuarra and he laughed.

"You see? I can go among the cities of Llarn in such a shape and everywhere I would be welcome."

"Until someone touched you," I remarked. "Illusions,

hallucinations—call them what you will—have no substance."

With a snarl twisting his lips, he put out his arm. "Touch it," he told me. "You, at least, I thought would understand. This is no phantom of your brain you see. When my body mutated during The War, it grew strange powers. I possess the telekinetic energies of mind over matter. I do not make you see me this way—I *am* this way, by a proper molding of the atoms and molecules of my body."

The twenty year old Kav Mork stood proudly, head thrown back. Under my hand his flesh was warm and tangible. He was no hallucination. He really was a handsome young man.

· "Then why—?"

His hand gestured. "Externals, externals! If I were to walk about this way, some jealous person might sink a dagger into me. Life is very precious to me, despite the fact that I have known so much of it. I go about as a khorl, knowing that men will draw back and away from me, leaving me safe to go about my business." His grin was sly. "However, there are times when I grow reckless, and become young and handsome in order to court some lovely woman of Llarn."

His eyes touched Tuarra, as if telling her she was such a woman who could tempt him from his role of khorl. When my hand fell on my daggerhilt, he laughed softly and, bending, picked up his black robe and put it about him.

"I have no taste for fighting and adventure. I leave that to others like yourself, Alan Morgan. I merely showed you that I can enjoy power and wealth as much as anyone."

He turned and walked out of the cabin into the night. I listened until his footfalls faded.

Tuarra was sitting very quietly, staring straight ahead of her. When my hand touched her shoulder, she shrank away from it.

"Please," she whispered. "Please. For all I know—you may be a khorl, too." She began to weep very quietly, bent forward with her face in her hands.

Her world had become a strange and terrible thing to Tuarra of Kharthol. It had lost its old, familiar outlines.

A little later she roused herself and shaking out her long black hair, rubbed away tears with the heels of her palms. She smiled at me from behind the heavy tresses through which she peeped.

"I must look a fright," she murmured.

"The loveliest fright I've ever seen," I grinned.

Her eyes fell before my look and she began tracing outlines in the thin dust on the cabin floor. Her moving finger touched off a thought in my head.

"Where are we on Llarn? Show me, Tuarra. Draw a map."

Her head nodded. I could not see her face through the spill of her heavy hair; I think she had loosed that hair deliberately to hide her features from me, for some womanly reason. But her finger began moving with purpose and soon I beheld dots that were cities and lines that showed continental masses, and the form of the twin oceans of Llarn.

"Here is Azorra, where the blue men live. Here—far away from Azorra, about five thousand erns—is Krondys on the southernmost tip of the Markoolian Sea."

"Is Markool one of the twin oceans?"

"Oh, no. The oceans are named Ytal and Okyl, after the gods of creation. Markool is one of the many seas that form the outer edges of the twin oceans."

"And where is Karthol?"

Her finger reached out and made a dot. "Far away, Alan Morgan. Fully ten thousand erns from Inislan to which we are bound." She made a tiny circle that represented the island to the north.

I studied the map a long time, listening to what she told me about Llarn, its cities and its land masses. The oceans were small, by Earth standards. Most of Llarn was land, great boundless stretches of grassland and baked desert and tableland. Much of it was unexplored, Tuarra admitted ruefully.

"Kharthol and a few other nations try to map out those unexplored regions but it is a hard task. There are unfriendly nations over much of them, that attack anyone flying above their territories. We have lost several scientific expeditions.

Now few men want to leave the security of Kharthol's walls."

She leaned her head onto my shoulder, apparently having forgotten that I might be a khorl. I put my arm about her shoulder and held her close.

A little later, she slept, rolled up in a fur pelt for warmth while I shuttered the bronze lamps so that only a faint radiance illuminated the room. By the brightness of the matter belt swinging lazily about the planet high above, I saw the robed form of Kav Mork standing at the black helm like a grim statue.

I took a long time to fall asleep. When I did, my dagger was naked in my fist. I too had lost a little trust in reality.

When I woke, the ship rolled easily to the surge of the waves. The grate of an anchor chain on wood was loud in the stillness. I came up on an elbow. The ship was not moving. Tuarra lay sleeping. Kav Mork stood in the open doorway, beckoning to me.

His finger pointed. I saw a low rocky island rising from the waves. There was snow on the tips of its low hills and ice glistened close to the shoreline where the seaform beat and clung.

"Inislan," he said softly, and his eyes glowed.

I made out through the mists the stone walls of what had once been a great citadel. It stood on a headland, towering above the sea pounding at the sheer cliff that formed its north wall. Its walls were stark, skeletal against the gray northern sky, with patches of that sky seen between openings that had once been windows. A desolate place, brooding agelessly beneath the cold white clouds that went scudding over its stones.

"You shall see it soon enough," he promised grimly, and turned toward the aft rail where a rope was knotted. "Give me a hand with the tender."

I put my palms to the heavy rope, grinning at him. "Why don't you use your powers to bring the boat alongside?"

He scowled. "My powers are not inexhaustible, just as your muscles are not tireless. Exerting telekinetic energy takes just as much out of me as hard work takes out of you. I save my strength for when it is most needed."

The rope was free. Together we tugged on it, drawing the slim tender alongside the mother ship. I put a hand on the rail, dropped lightly down onto a thwart under which two oars lay. A moment later, Kav Mork was beside me.

I rowed. Kav Mork sat in the bow, the tiller in a hand, steering the smallboat between the jagged rocks and up through the pounding surf onto a stoney beach. Pushing the boat onto the strand, we moved up along a slope toward the ruins of the citadel.

Kav Mork said breathlessly, "If the salorth doesn't appear, so much the better. You'll still have fullfilled your part of the bargain."

The sea birds cawed as they glided overhead beneath the swiftly moving clouds. The sky was gray, ominous. The rock was cold and wet underfoot as we walked, and a chill wind blew about our ankles, moving the thin stalks of dead flowers that rustled with a lifeless dryness. It was desolation, this place. Were it not for the ancient walls, I would have sworn that no man had ever before set foot on it.

Kav Mork touched my arm. "Wait here. I shall go below for what I seek. If the salorth comes—engage it with your sword. Hold it until I am safely out of the citadel and then come after me."

I waited, glancing across the rock wastes north of this headland. Some green mosses and some lichens showed, otherwise there was nothing, no sign of the salorth or even of its existence. Kav Mork walked rapidly, black robe swaying to his stride, past a standing wall and down onto a flight of stone steps that took him into the bowels of the island.

And then—

The island began to quake beneath me. It was as if its very bulk were shifting in some submarine disturbance. A wall of sound rose up about me as something bellowed an obscene hatred for all life but its own.

I whirled, my flesh cold, my heart hammering wildly, my

very blood seeming to congeal in my veins. Across the lichened rock of the island beyond the headland, a beast was coming at a shuffling run that covered ground like a galloping horse. Even as I drew my blade, I told myself nothing could be as horrible as this thing that ran for me with swift and terrible strides.

It was like a man, yet unlike a man. Humanoid in appearance with two legs and a torso to which were fitted two arms, it had an armored mouth and two eyes on stalks for a head, and thick scales over its entire body. It bellowed as it ran, and those bellows were what shook the island.

I could not take my eyes from it. I felt mesmerized, turned to stone as Earth legend said the Medusa turned men on whom it gazed to stone. Its long arms ended in two thick yellow claws that looked razorsharp. Once those claws dug into me, they would slice through my flesh as a warm knife cleaves through butter.

"Kav Mork—hurry!" I shouted.

My longsword looked puny in comparison with this monster bearing down on me. It stood twenty feet high, at least. Its arms must have been eight feet long. Every instinct told me to turn tail and run for the boat, but I could not leave the khorl.

I cried, "You must have found what you want by now. If you delay longer, neither of us will get away."

The thing was fifty feet away, then ten—

I lunged sideways as it came for me. I slashed down with my blade. Its edge sank deep and the monster hissed with pain. It turned its two red eyes toward me and opened its cavernous mouth. The roar that came from its chest came close to paralysing me with horror. Barely in time did I see the arm that slashed twin claws at me. I went back three feet, desperately glad that the lesser gravity of Llarn gave my Earth muscles increased strength and my body added speed and leaping power.

I snarled and drove in, slashing. I had never met anyone who could stand up to me with a sword in my fist, and I did not mean to find one now. Tuarra was in the black boat waiting for me. I meant to go back to her all in one piece.

My blade flew in a tangle of gray steel, making a web around the monster. It struck sparks where it glanced off its scaled torso, but where the scales were thin across its upper arm and neck my edge drew blood. I came in a second time and then a third. My blade went out and down. It cut through the upper arm of the beast, all the way through. The arm fell off.

I drew back, waiting for the thing to flee. It was grievously wounded. Blood was spurting from its empty armpit.

And then—

Even as I watched, it began to form another arm. No—two arms!

Swiftly did those arms grow! As I watched they extended grew big with scales and muscles and claws—

I leaped in, my blade swinging parallel to the rocky ground. Through the neck of the thing I drove my blade so that its head leaped upward off its shoulders. The headless trunk tottered on scaley legs.

And it grew two heads where one had been!

I think I went a little mad at that point. It was coming for me, mindless, idiotic, a life form created only to destroy other life forms. Its claws ripped into my arm, my leg, my side. Blood oozed from my sliced flesh. Weakness made my head buzz and my sight blur. I leaped, I staggered, I fought with my sword as never before.

It pressed me back against the rock. It came through the air, leaping. Its claws dug into the rock, slashing it. I shuddered. If the rocks had been my body it would have ripped my chest wide open. I wanted to be sick but there was no time. With my blade I had to fend off the salorth, keep it away from me.

I remembered Kav Mork but only dimly as in a dream. Had he emerged from the cellarways of the citadel with his treasure chest in his hands? Or did he cower there in horror of this mindless thing which even his powers could not control? I had no way of knowing.

All my senses were engrossed in the task of staying alive. The beast had four heads now and eight arms. It was monstrous, unbelievable. Whatever nuclear explosion had created it had performed a miracle.

Its arm drove against my chest, driving my back against the jagged edges of the rock where its claws had slashed. Claws that can cut through rock would have little trouble in destroying me. I braced myself, blade held out.

Then it came at me, even as I realized that my back was pressed against smooth stone, not jagged rocks. But this could not be! I slipped aside, ran eyes and the fingertips of my left hand over the rock. It was smooth, unmarred by so much as a scratch.

I backpedalled away from the monster. I wanted time to think. If there were no slash-marks in the stone, it meant—

I let my sword drop. The monster leaped.

I laughed and in midleap the thing dissolved into tenuous wisps of scale and flesh and claws that did not exist. Nothing touched me but the salt breeze moving over the rocky wastes of Inislan. The beast was gone.

No, not gone. It had, never existed!

I had been fighting a phantom, a mesmerization of an idea-image from the brain of Kav Mork. He had used his telekinetic energy to implant the idea of a monster called the salorth in my mind, in the nerve impulses and synapses of my cerebral cortex, making me envision what he wanted me to see.

I have no doubt but that I would have subconsciously willed myself to die, once those imaginary claws ripped into my flesh. As witch doctors can cause men to die on Earth, so the khorl could have caused me to die by implanting the mechanics of that death in my head.

I shuddered. Then anger grew in me, a hot tide of rage against Kav Mork. I whirled toward the cellarway passage into which he had disappeared. There was no sign of the khorl. I ran toward the spot, then halted suddenly.

71

My eyes lifted toward the Sea of Markool. It was empty. There was no sign of the black boat, nor of the tender.

I was alone on the island.

CHAPTER SIX

I RAN DOWN the rocky strand and into the water, staring with disbelieving eyes. There was no mistake. The sea was empty. There was no black boat, no lateen sail. I had been abandoned. As I felt loneliness move in me, I drew a deep breath and realized suddenly that the blood on my flesh and my wounds were gone.

They had never been, thanks to Kav Mork who had made me see what was not there and—

I brushed a hand before my eyes.

Now I noticed, after the first shock of abandonment, that the khorl must have prevented me from seeing things, as well. Here and there on the rocks jutting upward from the sea were the skeletal ribs of sunken vessels, ships driven onto this barren shore by storms while blown far off course. Those rocks past which he had steered while I rowed were festooned with broken spars and crushed keels and splintered hulls.

Hope moved in me for the first time. Perhaps somewhere on the island was a ship still staunch enough—or that could be made staunch with a little effort, with nails and tools brought from other wrecks—to carry me away from Inislan to . . .

To where?

Kav Mork had Tuarra in his power. At the thought my blood went cold but—even worse than that, I did not know where it was he intended taking her. Ah, but wait! He had mentioned wealth and power last night in the cabin when he had let us see him as a youth of twenty. There was only one place on Llarn where he could become rich and powerful through Tuarra of Kharthol.

In Kharthol itself.

The usurper Gorlun Duv would pay many golden torks to get his hands on the princess of Kharthol. To him, she represented the rightful rulership of that mighty metropolis. By wedding her, he would strengthen his illegal claim to its throne.

The treasure Kav Mork had sought here on Inislan had been of living flesh and blood, Tuarra of Kharthol herself. He got me out of the way by abandoning me, like the poor fool I was, fighting a monster that existed only in my imagination.

I wanted to kick myself around the island.

Instead I began to walk around it, on the beaches where I could set foot, or on the rocks that girdled its shores. My eyes hunted for smallboats or tenders, something I could sail with my own hands. Three times I plunged into the booming surf, three times I dragged boats onto the pebbled sands only to find them with their bottoms stove in, or otherwise useless.

Toward dusk I stumbled over part of a hull buried under sand. I went down on my knees, scrabbling with a hand and my dagger at the coarse grains. In half an hour I had uncovered enough of a tiny fishing smack to realize I could patch it up and take off in it. My spirits lifted as I crouched there, patting the wood as if it were the greatest treasure on two worlds.

Darkness was flooding the island when I came to my senses. I was hungry. I had not eaten all day. I rose to my feet, moving inland toward the mosses and the lichens. I knew nothing of Llarnian shrubs, or whether or not they were edible, and I did not mean to make the try. My stomach could do without food. But I needed water.

I found that water oozing out from the side of a sheer cliff face in a tiny trickle and I sat down there and sipped my fill. I watched the stars come out above me. I would sleep here the night and in the morning I would go back to where I had left the beach-buried fishing boat, uncover it, find oars from another wreck, and set off across the sea of Markool.

I had no idea where Kharthol might be, though I remembered that only the night before, Tuarra had drawn me a map of her world as she knew it. I tried to recall the outlines of the map she had scratched into the cabin dust.

I fell asleep, still taxing my memory.

In the morning I drank my fill of the cold, sweet water, then moved back toward the beach. I was a little more than halfway there when I saw the flier. It lay half-buried under soft loam and lichens, but I recognized its clean lines almost instantly. A flier would be infinitely faster than a small boat in getting me to Kharthol. I lifted my dagger to cut away the lichens that partially covered it.

When the flier lay exposed to the sunlight, I stared down at it in dismay. It was old. Old! Only Llarn knew how long it had lain here. Its lines were different from those of the flier on which Tuarra had flown to Paloranis and the fliers in which the four Khartholian soliders had followed her. What terrible storm had brought its owner down out of the sky so many years ago? Why had he not taken off again? I had no way of knowing.

All I had to know was whether the thing would fly.

I lay down on the flier and strapped myself on. I spent an hour studying its control levers. I might bang up against a rocky upthrust of the island as I took off, or swoop down into the sea before I was very high. I wanted to be absolutely certain I could operate the ship before I tried to fly, but I could not understand the Khartholian symbols worked into the control panel.

The only way to learn to fly was—to try.

I pressed a stud and felt a motor rumble into life. After the

74

first few shudders, it seemed to settle to a quiet susseration. Slowly I drew down on a lever. Instantly the flier rocked sideways. I reversed, tried another slot. The thing jumped, scraping its thin metal keel on the lichens. I sweated and swore, I banged my fist on the thin metal that strengthened its deckplanks.

My hand went out again. Gingerly I drew back on a white lever. The slender flier shook, righted itself and rose slowly upward. I pushed the white lever a little further and I went higher. I pushed the red lever. Slowly the flier began to move forward, always rising.

Triumph swelled my chest. I grinned through tight lips and started twisting the directional dials. In half an hour I felt I knew the controls of my little vessel. I made a wide circle above the island and turned its prow southward toward the warmer climes and—Kharthol.

I yanked the red lever to its last notch and clove the air of Llarn with all the speed its ancient motors could muster. About one hundred feet above the heaving waves of Markool I rode the wind like a frightened spirit. Southward, always southward I travelled with no sign of life anywhere below me.

Once I thought I saw something white moving in the green depths far below, but I could not be sure. Again, I caught glimpses of what seemed to be buildings far, far down along the ocean bottom, but this might have been a trick of the light and my own vision. I had not eaten in some time and an empty stomach will do things to a man's imagination.

A sail was a distant triangle of whiteness far off, and I saw the low, lean lines of what might have been a warship. Nothing else moved on the waves below me.

The isle of Inislan lay north-north-west of Kharthol by ten thousand erns, about fourteen thousand Earth miles, as close as I could figure by my own reckonings. Much of the sea of Markool lay between them, and a long stretch of lush grasslands where the herds of Kharthol and of Sarnak shared pasturage. Beyond this vast basin lay a fringe of foothills—

75

the Palnarrs, they are called—and a soggy marshland. Then the ground rose upward slowly to the heights on which Kharthol sprawled.

My flier was not the swift craft that Tuarra and her people knew today. It was centuries old as best I could judge, and it was slow. But it flew steadily, without yawing or pitching, and handled easily once I understood the knack of its dials and levers.

The sea fell away and now I saw distant herds of Llarnian cattle, great hoofed and horned animals renowned for the quality of their beef. Dusk found me still above those grasslands so I hunted out an area where the grass grew tallest and slid the flier into a safe hiding place.

I slept like a dead man.

My empty stomach waked me before the first red tints of dawn were in the air. It was ironic that I was within seeing distance of some of the greatest beef herds on the planet, yet I was close to starving. I tugged my kilt belt a notch tighter and revved up the flier's engine.

I flew as swiftly as I could, low to the ground, for I was approaching Kharthol with every ern I travelled, and I wanted to avoid being seen as long as possible. It was late afternoon when I swung past the last stretch of soggy marsh and headed toward the gradual uplift that would carry all the way to Kharthol.

When I saw the walls and towers of the city like a dot on the horizon, I dropped the flier to the ground. Not far off was a paved road twisting past a clump or rocks before turning straight toward the great Kartholian gate.

I set off at a good pace along the road. I had not gone very far when I saw a man sitting on a flat stone to one side of the road munching a fruit. Behind him was a tree heavy with these round red things that looked like peaches grown to the size of melons.

I had no money, but if he was the farmer who owned the fruit tree, I would offer to barter for it. I would not give up my longsword but my dagger was as good as money in my purse.

"How much?" I asked, gesturing at the tree.

He goggled at me, and his face looked as if he wanted to laugh, but was too polite. At last he shrugged and said almost apologetically, "I'm not in mood for humor, friend."

He finished the fruit and reached upward for another. I watched him with a dry mouth. My stomach was protesting almost audibly. I took out my dagger. He stopped eating to put his hand on his own hilt. I threw my dagger at his sandalled feet.

"A trade. My dagger for three fruit."

He squinted at me suspiciously, then his foot went out and kicked my blade back at me. "Where're you from? Hasn't Kharthol enough troubles without being inflicted with fools these days? Help yourself. The slinths are free. Always have been."

I picked a fruit before I retrieved my weapon. I ate hungrily, crudely, without caring that the stranger was looking me up and down, and at each new look grew even more curious. I ate four slinths before I sighed and wiped my hands on my thighs. The slinths were filling, having a rich, sweet pulp and plenty of juice to quench a thirst.

"Now then," I said to him, "what troubles has Kharthol these days?"

His scowl was black with suspicion. "You must be a Gorlun Duv spy," he growled, and got to his feet.

"I hate the man," I said lightly. "The only person in all Kharthol I care a snap of the fingers for is Tuarra, its princess."

He was still suspicious. "I suppose you've come to prevent her marrying the dagan," he commented sourly.

I was on my feet so fast that he blinked and took a step backward. "Marrying Gorlun Duv? Man, you lie."

"Ah, no. Why do you think I'm on my way to Kharthol now? Free wine, free food, free women. It's to be a holiday, starting today at sundown. The marriage takes place one trod from today."

I stood like an idiot, gaping at him. I told myself I had known this was to happen. It was the reason Kav Mork had abandoned me on Inislan. Yet to be faced with the reality was something else again. One thing I gave the khorl: he wasted no time.

"Where is Kav Mork now?" I asked dully.

The man leaned forward, staring. "What know you of Kav Mork the khorl? I thought only a handful were aware of how he delivered the princess of Kharthol over to her enemy! I know because my sister is to work on the wedding garments as she told me yestereday when she paid her weekly visit to the farm where I live."

I gestured him to sit down. I told him the whole story of how I met Tuarra in Paloranis and of how we were captured by the Azunn, of our escape with the help of the khorl, and my abandonment of Inislan. He listened quietly, nodding occasionally.

For the first time he smiled at me with open honesty. "Your tale tallies exactly with that of the princess. My sister and I—together with Gorlan Duv and the rest of Kharthol —did not believe her tale of a swordsman who defeated all four of the men Gorlun Duv sent to bring her back. They were great warriors. For one man to defeat them all in fair fight—"

He broke off to stare hard at me. "I suppose you have some hare-brained scheme to rescue Tuarra from her marriage commitment?"

"If I can. I certainly mean to try."

"She thinks you're dead, you know. The last she saw of you was when you were fighting some invisible demon on Inislan."

"It was visible to me—for a time. It's true that Tuarra would not have been able to see it, because my own mind had conjured it up." I explained what Kav Mork had done to me.

78

My new friend rose to his feet, gesturing at the road. "Come, we will walk toward Kharthol and as we walk I shall tell you of the city and explain why you have absolutely no chance to rescue the princess."

He spoke heavily, with hopelessness in his voice. I gathered that he would gladly help me if he saw any chance of success. He agreed he would, even though he risked the enmity of Gorlun Duv for his part in the conspiracy.

His name was Barrluk Tann. He was the only son and the heir of the wealthiest cattle herder on the Khartholian grasslands. He and his father would have honored posts at the wedding ceremony and later at the feasting. He was in Kharthol now, he explained, to make some purchases as well as enjoy himself.

"There is to be a nuptial parade this afternoon, when Tuarra will be carried though the main thoroughfares of the city to be shown to the people. It's an old custom and will give you the chance at least to lay eyes on her before she's married."

It would give me a chance to abduct her, too.

His face was horrified. "Abduct her? Out of Kharthol? Man, you're mad! Nothing can save her, now Gorlun Duv has her in his grasp."

I said thoughtfully, "What kind of ruler was Tuarra's father, Drakol Tu?"

"A good man, loved by everyone."

"Strange then, that Gorlun Duv was able to seize the throne."

"Gorlun Duv was general of the army. It was a military coup, the troops in Kharthol proper giving him their allegiance. Oh, the usurper isn't so secure on the throne that Drakol Tu couldn't oust him, once Drakol Tu comes out of hiding, wherever he is—"

"He's a prisoner of the Azunn."

Barrluk Tann whistled. "No wonder he hasn't shown himself. All Kharthol waits for him to appear, to set up his standard in the field against that of Gorlun Duv. Clever, clever.

Gorlun Duv keeps him out of the way while he strengthens his grip on the throne by wedding the daganna."

"If I could get Tuarra out of Kharthol—somehow set Dra-ol Tu free—rouse up an army . . ."

"You dream," he snorted, and we walked on in silence.

The more I thought of it, the more impossible it became. But it had been considered impossible to escape the Azunn, yet here I was, a free man on my way to find the girl I loved. It had been next to impossible to get off the isle of Inislan, but I had done it. I tightened my lips.

Somehow, I would find a way.

The city of Kharthol sprawls over half a hundred trogs. It is an ancient city, one of the oldest on all Llarn. It was the only city that had fought in The War and still was a planetary power. And it was the home of Tuarra. I studied its high red walls, its great towers—slim and delicate, like faery turrets against the sky, four in number and each a duplicate of the others—as Barrluk Tann and I advanced on the great Khartholian Gate.

We were joined now by other travellers, all on foot or riding in small covered wagons drawn by striped drals. It was a law in Kharthol that none could enter its gates except on foot or in these little carts that trundled along so easily on their big tires. On every road into Kharthol, Barrluk Tann informed me, way stations were set up that were like small towns, where drals and larger vehicles were left behind while their owners went into Kharthol on foot or in rented wagons.

There was an air of gaiety, of holiday about the people. They were dressed in bright kilts, in jackets of many hues. They laughed and talked together, stranger with stranger, and greeted us with shouts and ribald remarks. Barrluk Tann and I agreed that we would keep my secret, and so he introduced me, when we met Khartholians he knew, as a new helper among his grassland herders. I noted that every man carried a sword at his side. Most of them, I assumed, were able to use them with some degree of skill.

Barrluk Tann explained to me, when I questioned him, that during the long centuries after The War, every male who survived became a warrior out of necessity. Now the male population of great city-nations like Kharthol required military service of all its male inhabitants. The War and its hard aftermath had weeded out all who were not fighting men. Today a man gloried in the knowledge that he could handle himself almost as well as a trained soldier in the event of a fight.

I was pleased at this news. It would make it harder for Gorlun Duv to remain dagan once Drakol Tu made a move to regain his throne. Barrluk Tann pointed out to me gloomily that once the usurper married Tuarra, he would be accepted as dagan readily enough; even if Drakol Tu should return to the throne, Gorlun Duv would be his dragor, the crown prince next in line to succeed to the title.

It was not pleasant information.

As we heared the lively music that heralded the coming of the wedding paraders, I told myself that I must get Tuarra out of Kharthol at all costs. I watched impatiently for her carriage, paying little or no attention to the mounted troops on striped drals, the marching foot soldiers who served on the big battle-fliers that darkened the sky above Kharthol as they cruised back and forth, displaying the colors of the daganna.

The swelling murmurs of the crowd told me Tuarra was approaching long before I saw the white carriage in which she sat upright, with her eyes fixed straight ahead. She was robed in white fur and scarlet cloth, and there was a slender golden fillet on her thick black hair. She had never looked more regal. I gawked like a lovestruck youth before I remembered why I was here.

"Alan Morgan," I cried out. "Alan Morgan loves you!"

Tuarra reacted as if struck across the face. She went white, then red, and seemed to shrink a little inside her ornate robes. Then her green eyes were scanning the crowd as her lovely lips parted to aid her rapid breathing.

81

I had taught my princess very little of my own language but that much at least she understood. I took out my sword, yelling, "For Tuarra of Kharthol!"

Only Tuarra understood the words, but everyone understood the gesture. Swords rose into the air to form a steel forest through which I fought my way to her carriage. Her eyes misted in tears as she stared down at me. Her little hand came out to catch mine. I kissed it, almost forgetting the words I must speak to her before we parted.

"Where can I see you?"

"The palace gardens, at the bridge gate."

"Tonight?"

"At the hour of the dral," she whispered.

The press of the sword tore us apart as half a dozen troopers forced their way to the carriage to keep it moving. I fell back throught the press, hunting for Barrluk Tann. Side by side we thrust our way into an empty side street where I told him what had happened.

"The hour of the dral is long past sundown, even past the dining hour here in Kharthol," he informed me. "We have plenty of time to choose a sleeping establishment and make arrangements for our evening meal."

When I explained I had no money, he swayed in great good humor. "I have more money than I can possibly use. Willingly would I pay ten thousand torks to any man able to prevent Tuarra from marrying Gorlun Duv. Consider this a loan, if you will."

He pushed half his coins at me, making me weight down the leather purse that is a part of every Llarnian kilt-belt. He explained that the currency of Kharthol was the same as every other city-nation of the golden skinned Vrann. A tork was the standard unit of money, being a gold coin about the size of an American half dollar. Then was the anth, worth half a tork, a quinn, a quarter of its value, and the cheaper durk, worth only an eighth its value. He had shoveled approximately twenty torks into my purse.

Since it cost two durks for sleeping silks and possibly five durks for a heavy meal, my coins would keep me fed and rested for a long time to come.

"And if you need money after your attempt to abduct the daganna fails—come see me at my cattle house. That is, if you're still alive."

We found a public house not far from the palace itself, in a neighborhood of old houses run to seed and converted into shops and taverns. Barrluk Tann explained that less than half an hour's walk would bring me close to the palace gardens and the bridge gate. Then we set out to eat.

For the first time I tasted Khartholian beef and understood its reputation in the more civilized cities of Llarn. A thick steak and freshly baked bread, with two beakers of strong white wine, and I felt I could take on Gorlun Duv's army by myself.

Barrluk Tann grinned at me.

"You attempt the impossible, you know."

I smily wryly. "It is impossible for me to be on this planet, yet I'm here." I frowned and lifted out the metal ball I had taken from the black altar. It lay on my palm, winking in the overhead lamps. Barrluk Tann leaned closer, frowning.

"Have you ever seen anything like it?" I asked.

"Never. It seems like a toy the children use in a game they call 'graddy'—but it is not quite metal, not quite glass. There seem to be strange depths to it."

I sighed and put the ball away. We talked on over cups of steaming lakk, which is a drink resembling coffee laced with a stimulant. It is much favored in all the cities of the gold-skinned peoples. I found it flavorful and enjoyable. It was Barrluk Tann who rose to his feet first.

"The hour of the dral approaches, Alan Morgan."

My heart was starting to hammer inside my chest. Soon now I would hold my precious Tuarra against me and kiss the lips I loved. It did not occur to me that I would be in any danger. I was going to see Tuarra, to sweep her up in my arms and carry her out of Kharthol to safety. This was as far as my thoughts went, if indeed they went farther than the moment when I would hold her in my arms.

Such is the way of lovers. There are no obstacles, no barriers in their paths: the loved one is the only one who matters. Let the devil take Gorlun Duv! For I meant to have Tuarra.

Barrluk Tann and I said our farewells on a corner under a lithium lamp. These little lamps are coated with lithium treated in such a manner that they glowed brightly in the nighttime hours and fade to insignificance in daylight. They are a more modern adaptation of the glowing metal strips I found in the museum at Azorra.

I turned and walked away.

The darkness and the shadows from the lithium lamps stretched ahead of me. There were few strollers at this hour, and none but myself so close to the high stone walls of the palace gardens. It seemed that my footsteps echoed from paving stone to wall and—

You are here on Llarn! Ahhh. . . .

I went on walking, almost automatically. Inside my chest my heart was pumping wildly. The voice had come to me! After such a long time, it had spoken once again.

I was weak. It took more energy than I supposed to wrench you out of your space-time continuum and through hyperspace here to Llarn. Much, much more.

Somewhere I head a nightbird calling. Soon I would see Tuarra.

You are to come to me. Quickly, quickly—for I am very weak!

I thought, "I cannot! I go to rescue the woman I love."

Love? What is love to me? Come, as I have bidden you!

"I cannot. First I must save Tuarra."

Tiny little tendrils moved in my brain. I felt them lightly, as if mist might have substance, questing, thrusting. A weight rested there, slowing my walk, bringing me to a halt. I stood quivering, understanding that the voice had put a part of itself inside me, in some strange joining.

And then, slowly, the voice spoke again.

I had—forgotten. It has been so long that I knew aught of humankind, its love and hates and how precious each are to them.

There was sadness in it as the voice went on whispering.

I am sorry. Truly sorry. But my life force itself depends on what you do, and swiftly. You have the elathin, the metal ball. You will bring it to me.

Now!

I turned around and retraced my steps like a dead thing, a zombie, without will. My heart and my mind went on ahead of me to the palace gardens and the bridge gate where Tuarra was waiting for me to come to her. My flesh and my muscles walked through the Khartholian night, intent only on leaving the city, on travelling where the voice wanted me to travel.

I walked out through the great Khartholian gate minutes before it closed for the night. The guards looked at me oddly—nobody ever left Kharthol at such an hour!—but they passed me through readily enough. If I was a madman, I would be better off outside the city than in.

I walked until I came to my flier. I dragged off the boughs and branches with which I had hidden it, and lay down and strapped myself to it. My hands fumbled with the controls.

An instant later the flier was lifting, circling to avoid the upper reaches above Kharthol that are heavily guarded during the night, then moving at top speed southwestward. I flew high at the bidding of the voice, for there are low mountains between Kharthol and the region of Llarn toward which I flew.

The flier was an old one, but its motor was still in good running condition. I cleaved the upper air of Llarn like a disembodied spirit, hurtling over the grasslands and the dead sea bottoms that stretch from Kharthol south toward what was once Meradion.

All night I ran before the wind, and into the next day.

The voice did not speak again, but it was in my mind, for when I would have reversed the controls to return to Kharthol, it prevented me.

I suffered untold agonies of spirit during that long night. What would Tuarra think when I failed to show up at our rendezvous? In despair, believing me dead, she might wed Gorlun Duv. I hammered my fist on the metal control strip until the edge of my hand was raw, but always the flier raced on, away from the girl I loved.

Daylight found me moving over a vast and uninhabited region that showed no sign of life or even of one-time habitation. It was a dead and barren landscape below, affording not even a glimpse of a berry bush. Only baking sand and red clay and gray rock could be seen from horizon to horizon.

The sun cooked my back as the flier raced southward. Only when dusk came was there any relief from it. Now the voice whispered to my mind and my hand obeyed its orders. I swung the directional lever of the flier sideways and the little ship responded by veering to the west. I was exhausted by this time; I had been awake for hours. As though it wanted me fresh and able to fulfill its will, the voice began touching those edges of my brain that controlled my sleep responses. My head fell forward. I slept.

I woke to another day, and a vast stretch of mossy ground that gave way to gradually rising uplands, to a plateau that was covered with trees and thick green grasses. Halfway through the day, I saw something up ahead.

I lifted on an arm, peering forward.

There were men far below, moving about as though fighting. Wondering whether the voice would stop me, I touched the controls, slowing my little craft, dipping it lower and lower until its keel almost scraped the treetops. Now I had a better look at those moving figures.

There were three blue men and more than a dozen creatures attacking them. Azunn men I had seen before, so my gaze was directed mainly at their opponents.

They were tall, perhaps seven feet or more, and heavy

86

in proportion. Each wielded a longsword with which he drove the blue men back and back toward the wreckage of a wagon. They did not seem to be trying to kill the blue men. They fought warily and with caution, as if they wanted to exhaust and capture them.

I owed the Azunn nothing. They are a cruel people and little loved anywhere on Llarn. Accordingly, I was reaching for the speed controls to fly on and away from them when I saw one of their attackers swing a blade and knock off a helmet worn by a blue warrior. Instantly a spill of black hair tumbled down to the hips of the Azunn.

A woman!

I rasped a curse under my breath. I waited for the voice to take command of my body, to prevent me from slowing the flier and turning it in a long curve to land. I could not let a woman, even an Azunn woman, face such danger without lifting my blade to protect her. Nor did the voice stop me as the keel bumped the grasses and I was off the flier with my sword in my hand, racing toward the struggling fighters.

Even as I ran I saw two bodies—blue bodies—lying on the ground to one side. The Azunn were paying a high price for having been discovered on these grasslands. Just as I came up with them, another blue man dropped.

I ran my blade into two of their attackers before they realized I was there. Three of them turned, slashing down at me with their long blades, but I was under them, thrusting, stabbing sideways, before their steel could touch me.

I leaped away, came in again.

My blade flew like a living thing. I controlled it almost in some symbiotic manner, as though it were a part of me. I can never explain my ease with a sword; it may be a throwback to my former existence as a fighting man in some previous life. I am not much on explanation. I accept the reality for what it is, and I am grateful.

I parried and thrust. I leaped and bounded back and forth, away from savage slashes. I bent low before vicious thrusts. Five of the attackers were down when I felt soft flesh touch my arm and found the blue woman close beside me.

"You are a demon, Alan Morgan," she breathed.

I turned in surprise to find myself staring into the lovely face of Ulazza. I was so stunned I almost forgot to parry, so that I came close to taking a cut in my upper arm.

As I fought on, I panted, "What is the sister of Morlan Az doing out of Azorra?"

"For that matter, what are you?" she wondered, and I caught a little of the awe and fright in which she held me. No prisoner had ever escaped the Azunn before. Yet I, with Tuarra, had slipped from their city as easily as if we had been ghosts. In a sense, we had been, with the help of the khorl.

There was no time for further talk. The last blue man was down and I was facing half a dozen of these tall grass-land savages whom I learned from Ulazza were called yuuls. They were fair swordsmen, but I was a master. I rushed them, my blade dipping and darting. I was in front of them and on their flank and then behind them in a matter of seconds. One went down with my point in his throat, another with cold steel in his middle. A third fell as I slashed at his throat.

The yuuls were fighters, as are most Llarnians. They never knew the word fear or surrender. With the sun broiling me, with the sweat running down my back and down my sides, I battled without rest.

My blade flew in and out like a shuttle. It flashed redly and drops of blood flew from its tip. From time to time I caught glimpses of Ulazza staring at me with wide eyes as if she could not credit what she was seeing. The clanging of the blades, the heat and the dust around us, the contorted features of the yuuls as they fought savagely and the awed eyes of the blue woman, were forever imprinted on my memory.

A last yuul and I faced each other with out blades ringing. He was the most adept swordsman of them all. He fought a delaying battle, making a shrill whistling sound with his mouth all the time.

I heard Ulazza scream, "He is signalling! Hurry—destroy him!"

I sprang forward. My point dipped past the guard of his sword. It drew blood. The yuul was badly wounded but it was still sending out that high-pitched call. I had no way of knowing how long it would take others of its kind to reach us, but instinct told me to end the fight soon.

I parried, I riposted, I lunged.

His sword came up, awkwardly. My point drove past his hilt, deep into his chest between two ribs. The yuul stood a moment, gasping, before it plunged forward and lay face-down without moving.

Ulazza was running toward me, black hair flying. "Quickly, quickly. There'll be others all around us very soon. We've got to get away."

I caught her hand, drew her at a run beside me toward the flier. The ship was built to hold one person; I had no way of knowing whether it would carry both of us. All I could do was try.

I strapped her on, and then myself. My hand touched the controls. When I heard Ulazza gasp, I looked back and saw three yuuls on striped drals galloping toward us. I shoved the lever on full lift and ground my teeth together.

The flier rose slowly, lazily. Its motor quivered with the unaccustomed weight, but it responded. Upward it slipped, gathering a little speed. Ulazza put her head on the warm metal of the control plate, and shuddered. It had been a close call.

One of the yuuls reined in and lifted a long-barreled ray-rifle. A thin red beam sped upward. I yanked off my kranth—that medallion which absorbed the power of the red rays—and watched the beam hit it and rebound harmlessly. Then the flier was fully a hundred feet above the ground and moving steadily out of range of the needle rays.

I increased the speed lever and the flier responded sluggishly. It went no faster than a dral might do at the gallop, and for a while the three yuuls stayed with us, firing from time to time.

"What am I going to do with you?" I asked Ulazza.

She turned and stared at me through the falling flood of her hair. There was calculation in her eyes, and something like laughter. Her lips quivered into a smile.

"Take me to Azorra. What else?"

"And be tortured to death by Morlan Az? How is he?"

"Alive and well, having come out of the coma in which he was in, so that our physicians could heal him."

"I suppose he can't wait to get his hands on me."

"You saved me from the yuuls." She shivered and her lips twisted grotesquely in sudden fright. "The yuuls hate the Azunn. When they capture one of us, they execute us publicly, making a festival of it. It—takes a long time to die when the yuuls are doing the torturing."

"You blue-skins have a similar reputation."

"It is not at all the same," she flared. "We execute by torture to appease the spirits that are inside every man. This way we do away with the insult to our honor."

I grunted. She eyed me, then said, "You have no need to fear death if you take me back to Azorra. I swear it. Morlan Az has always done what his siter Ulazza has asked him to do. I will ask him to spare you life, to honor you."

Her hand touched mine. There was a plea in her black eyes that my own eyes could not meet. I let my gaze move below the flier along the grasslands and the distant foothills to the south. There was movement off to one side as a tawny animal fully three feet high at the shoulder moved through the underbrush.

"An aporad," Ulazza whispered. "They roam the plains. They are great meat eaters." Her voice told me she would not survive more than an hour were I to put her down anywhere short of Azorra.

"We hunt them," she went on. "I was hunting them when

90

the yuuls surprised us. The yuuls consider aporad meat a great delicacy. We kill them to protect our herds on which they prey. Not—to eat them."

The distaste in her voice told me she considered the yuuls to be sub-human, just as Tuarra considered the blue people to be far below her. The flier made a shadow near the big cat, causing it to lift its great maned head and open a mouth ringed with two sets of fangs above and below its tongue. To a man on foot, the aporad would be a formidable opponent.

"A dral can outrun it," Ulazza explained, "which is why all our hunting parties go mounted."

I said nothing more, keeping the flier pointed steadily westward. I had no idea where Azorra lay until the woman spoke again.

"You are flying too far south," she said softly.

"I don't intend to put myself in your brother's power, Ulazza. Understand that. I'll let you off somewhere close to Azorra—"

No, Alan Morgan. Take her into the city itself.

I went rigid. Ulazza felt my muscles tense and stared at me. I had forgotten the voice in the excitement of the battle with the yuuls. Now it was ordering me to commit suicide.

Not suicide, no. There is in the cellars of Azorra a rod that you must fetch and bring to me. Reset your controls. It was time you did this, in any event.

I thought, "The Azunn will slay me. If you can read my mind as I think you can, you must know what has happened to me on Llarn."

I know. But, you will be safe.

Well, the voice had its own reasons for commanding me to go to Azorra. I tried to appease my anxiety by telling myself that the voice would let nothing happen to me until I fulfilled its mission.

Unless it blacked out again.

91

CHAPTER SEVEN

ULAZZA WATCHED with wide eyes as I corrected my controls, moving the flier a few degrees north by northwest. I knew she wondered at my change of heart but she said nothing, only settling down on the flier to a more comfortable position beside me, cupping her chin on her hands and staring straight ahead as though expecting to see Azorra lift from the grasses at any moment. Her silence gave me time to think about Tuarra.

I had no way of knowing Llarnian marriage customs, but I assumed that Gorlun Duv would be as eager a bridegroom as any man back on Earth; besides, he was marrying Tuarra not for love but for reasons of politics.

He would not let himself be put off very long. Soon, very soon, Tuarra would become queen of Karthol. And—out of my reach forever!

"You think glum thoughts," Ulazza said gently.

She had turned her head and was resting her cheek on the back of a hand as she regarded me. I did not like what I could read in the depths of her black eyes. They were not threatening. On the contrary, they seemed quite friendly.

I told her about Tuarra being the prisoner of Gorlun Duv, and how he intended to marry her. Ulazza laughed when I finished.

"You rescued her from us only to give her to your rival. It's ironic, isn't it?" She hesitated, then added, "The sun of Llarn does not rise and set on Tuarra of Kharthol alone. There are other women on Llarn."

She managed to preen lying flat on her stomach on the cramped deck of the little flier, patting her black hair with her fingertips, letting me see the languid droop of her red mouth and long eyelashes. She was a beautiful woman and the extremely pale blue tint of her skin gave her an exotic loveliness that was not lost on me.

But I happed to love Tuarra.

I would have told her so except that I saw the pink and red and brown stones of Azorra lift from the undulating hills that were its homeland. It was a brilliant sight in the sunlight, and I felt as one of the mariners of the planet's ancient past might have when he sighted it from his topmast. To him it had been a stopover between anchorings, and no more than a port of call. It might turn out to be my grave.

I said, as I dropped the little craft half a mile from the great gate, "Remember your promise of safe conduct, Ulazza."

"No harm shall come to Alan Morgan in Azorra," she exclaimed proudly.

Half a hundred dral riders burst from the opening gate toward us, brandishing their weapons. They had seen the color of my skin and took me for an enemy. When Ulazza rose and let drop her silks to show her pale blue body, their cries turned to curious stares. They reined their striped mounts in and came forward at a canter.

When they recognized Ulazza, they stopped and stared. One of them, an older man with the badges of his rank as torgan clear to read on his horns, dismounted and walked forward, palm uplifted. His eyes went to the sister of his dagan, then to me. Puzzlement was written large on his face.

"Tell my brother I have returned to Azorra with the man who saved my life from the yuuls," Ulazza said slowly.

She turned and held out her hand. It was a peace gesture. or so I understood it to be; I caught her hand in mine and walked with her into the city. The mounted escort trailed at our heels.

The people came crowding the streets, leaving a narrow lane for us to move. It was the first time in all their history that a man with white skin had walked freely and of his own will, not a prisoner nor dead, into their midst. They made no sound. They merely stared and nudged one another.

The farther we walked, the greater the crowds became, until by the time we were ascending the stone steps of the black marble palace of Morlan Az, they made a living carpet on every avenue leading into the great square. The square itself was filled with the blue people. On all sides we could hear the buzz and mumble of their conversation.

"You've made history this day," I muttered to Ulazza.

"I shall make more history for the Azunn before I'm done," she flashed at me with an enchanting smile.

Her little horns caught the sunlight, sparkled where they had been gilded. Then the bronze doors were opening and the dimly lit interior of the hall was before us. Ulazza firmed her fingers on mine, almost tugging me forward.

I could see Morlan Az seated upright on the golden throne beyond the painted pillars between which we walked. His eyes were hard, his face seemed carved from sapphire. His horns were larger than the tiny nubs of Ulazza, giving him the appearance of a human bull. I tried to read emotion in his face and eyes, but there was only a hard coldness there.

He inclined his head to Ulazza, saying, "Welcome to the sister of Morlan Az My torgan has informed me that this enemy of our people save your life. Is it true?"

Ulazza burst out with a rhapsodic description of my fight with the yuuls. She described my swordsmanship in terms that brought a flush to my cheeks. She told how they had been hunting the aporad on the yuulian grasslands, how the yuul had charged them, how her escort had fought for their lives and her own. Then she had seen my flier.

"He could have gone on and left me to die there. He did not. He landed and with his sword killed the yuuls who would have taken me for their torture killing."

She went on speaking, and I thought I saw a change come over the face of Morlan Az. The hardness of his face softened slightly; he nodded his head from time to time, and his eyes, when he glanced at me, were not the hot hellholes they had been.

Ulazza ended by saying, "I have promised him immunity from your vengeance, my brother. I have given my royal word that he will not be harmed."

"You had not the right to make the promise, Ulazza," Morlan Az said gently. "In all things I agree with you but—not this."

Hie eyes searched her face for understanding and a memory came to me that once Tuarra had told me that the ruler of the Azunn had but a single weakness. She had spoken a word that I did not know. Su'ur. Sister. The Sister of Morlan Az was his only Achilles' heel. For her he would do anything. Well, almost anything. He would not forgive me for having struck him, for having shamed him before his soldiers and his people.

"It is not my honor that demands it as much as it is the honor of the throne," he said softly. "As a man I gladly forgive him, but as dagan of the Azunn, such forgiveness is not in my power."

Ulazza quivered beside me. I heard her harsh breathing. Glancing sideways I saw her eyes narrow, her nostrils flare in excited anger. Morlan Az seemed troubled. Evidently he had experienced his sister's anger before, and did not like it.

"Morlan Az speaks words," she snapped, "that come not from his heart but from his brain. He makes excuses to salve his pride as a warrior, not as dagan of the Azunn. He should know by this time that it is no disgrace to fall victim to the greatest warrior Azorra has ever known!"

The dagan squirmed. His soldiers, lined in ranks on either side of the great golden throne, and his courtiers behind us, did not move or speak, but the dagan was wondering what they thought of a ruler who would take such a tongue-lashing from a woman.

Ulazza gestured. "What man among all of you could defeat a dozen yuuls by himself? Were it not for Alan Morgan

95

I would be a yuul prisoner, marked for death by shameful tortures. Is this how Ulazza is loved in Azorra?"

She turned to me, held out her hand. "Come, Alan Morgan. We will leave Azorra together."

Morlan Az was on his feet, white and furious.

"Ulazza! I forbid it!" he shouted.

She did not look at him. Instead her fingers curled about mine and tugged. Grinning to myself, I went with her back down the aisle. The courtiers parted to make way for us.

"Arrest the man!" the dagan bellowed. "By force if necessary. But—do not harm Ulazza."

"Shall I fight?" I asked her.

She shook her head. "No, Alan Morgan. Though you kill a hundred Azunn, the result would only be the same. There is another way. Say nothing, just follow my lead."

She swung about and looked at the throne. "Know, Morlan Az, that such punishment as you mete out to Alan Morgan shall also be mine. I vow this—on the golden horns of the great god Kann."

The room was deathly still as Ulazza unhooked my sword and handed it to the panar, or lieutenant, of the guard. She said clearly, "The cell that holds this man will also hold the daganna of Azorra."

We walked from the throne room side by side, the guards all around us, while Morlan Az raged on the golden throne. He choked on the commands that should have brought Ulazza back to him. His lips twisted around the words that would have ordered his men to separate us. He knew only too well that no blueskin would touch Ulazza with force.

Down into the cellars below the palace we were taken, to a great chamber barred on two sides, with two stone walls hung with tapestries, with a table and chairs and a great soft couch. When I commented on the luxury of the room as the cell door slammed shut behind us, Ulazza smiled wanly.

"Only state prisoners are kept here. To my knowledge,

only one man was ever put in it. My uncle, when he rebelled against my father, long ago."

Her eyes stared up at me in mute appeal. "You should have been thrown in a mean hole, dark and damp. Knowing I would have gone in there with you, the guard took us here. But it is none the less a prison."

I chuckled. She frowned, "You think it funny?"

"No, only opportune. As daganna you can command a royal feast for us, can't you? You can order weapons to be brought to you."

She smiled a little, brightening. "I suppose so, yes."

"You can also demand that you be given a key to the cell bars, in case you decide to change your mind and leave."

She gasped, "Of course! We can walk out at any time. I should have thought of that, myself."

"It won't be all that easy," I admitted grudgingly. "We don't know the cellar layouts, there'll be guards posted to keep me in the cell, and Morlan Az, when he makes up his mind what to do with me, will come himself and hold you with his own hands while I'm taken out to be killed."

Her features seemed to crumple. Tears misted her great dark eyes. The hand she put on my forearm trembled. "I knew all that. I was hoping against hope that I could be wrong."

"We must plan," I said.

"If only there were hope."

"A man makes his own hope," I told her.

I made her lie down on the couch to rest while I explained what I wanted her to do. First, she must leave the cell, using as an excuse the fact that she wanted a change of clothing. She must find an old plan of the cellars, probably in the Hall of Dead Things, and commit it to memory. Better yet, she could attempt to smuggle it into the cell with her garments.

Before I was done, the pleasure was back in her face.

"Yes," she nodded. "It could be done that way. Oh, yes —it's certainly worth the try."

She swung off the couch, went to the bars and began calling for the guard. The panar in command came and with his own key opened the cell door for her. His expression said he had won a bet that she would not spend more than a few minutes in here with me.

Ulazza remained away so long I began to fear that the young officer had read her better than I. But when she finally appeared, she came laden with expensive gowns, with platters heaped high with steaming meats and chilled fruit, with maps and weapons smuggled in among her wearing apparel. It made me smile to see the dumbfounded expression on the face of the panar as his daganna entered my cell once more. I suppose he was seeing the loss of a hundred quinns.

First we feated on roast bork steak and cold strimth, a kind of fruit that resembles an orange. Then Ulazza spread out the cellar maps she had taken from the Hall of Dead Things. Quickly she pointed to the cell in which we were imprisoned, and her fingernail traced a course of possible escape among the underground corridors.

Not that way, man of Earth! Remember the rod of taliforr!
The voice was with me again. I had forgotten it in the worry over my plight, here in Azorra. I thought, "What rod of taliforr? And where shall I find it in this maze of tunnels?"
The rod can be found under the Temple of Arone.

I found the Temple after a long study of the map, and pored over the intersecting tunnels that moved through its cellars. Yes, by making a slight detour, I could reach that chest, remove the rod and add it to the metal ball in my purse.

I rolled up the maps and put them in my weapons belt. Ulazza was watching me with overbright eyes, a pucker of worry between her thin black brows.

"When shall we go, Alan Morgan?"

Her hand came up to stroke my neck, tracing the line of my jaw. Her fingertips quivered as they ran across my lips. She was very near, soft and warm, and she was a most beautiful woman. I could read the tenderness in her eyes.

"Only say the word, Alan Morgan, and there will be no need to flee through the cellarways."

When I began to speak, however, she put her fingers over my mouth, smiling roguishly. "No, wait. Before you say anything let me explain that were you to wed with me you would be adopted into the Azunn. You would be a prince-consort, mate to a princess. You would be highly honored. A warrior such as you would be a most welcome member of the blueskins."

"It cannot be, Ulazza."

Her thin black brows drew together as the devilfires touched her proud eyes. "It's that Khartholian princess, isn't it?" she hissed.

"I love Tuarra, yes."

Her hands made claws as she lifted them. I think for a moment she meant to hurl herself at me, to run those finger-nails down my cheeks in a fury that might match the savagery of an aporad. But slowly the devilfires faded out, and she looked sad and lonely.

"I knew you loved her. I told myself that—that perhaps it was not a true love, that I could win you for myself. I still think I can, if I can be with you more than I have been. So—I will come with you."

The woman must not come! Tell her. . . .

I said, "Ulazza, you know by this time that I come from a planet called Earth. You do not know how or why I came to Llarn. Let me explain."

I told her about the voice I had heard all my life, how the voice had lifted me off Earth and transported me across an inconceivable distance to this planet that was her home. I took out the metal ball and let her see it. Then I explained that I must get a rod of a strange substance and with the rod, bring it to the voice.

She was shivering when I finished.

Suddenly she covered her face with her hands, so that her gilded horns protruded between her spread fingers. Her voice was muffled when she spoke, and I knew that she was weeping.

"An ephelos, an ephelos," she sobbed. "It will kill you!"

When I protested, she lowered her hands and stared at me with horrified eyes. "You do not understand! An ephelos cannot help but kill a human being. It gives off—gives off a . . ."

"Radiation?" I asked, feeling cold.

She nodded. "Yes, a radiation—fatal to our form of life. Long ago, after The War, when the blue apes evolved into the Azunn, the epheloin were born. I don't understand it all but something in their genes was so affected by the radioactivity which bathed all Llarn that—they too evolved, into something not-man.

"At first there were many of them, then they grew fewer and fewer in number. I don't know why. Nobody does. Nobody could ever get close enough to find out. Anyone who did see an ephelos grew great lesions on his skin and died in agonized convulsions not long afterward."

Her hand touched mine. "Please, Alan Morgan. Stay here in Azorra. I am sure my brother will forgive you. Stay with me."

I shook my head. "I cannot. Even if I would, the voice won't let me. It is here," I tapped my head, "inside my mind. It made me walk out of Kharthol when I was on my way to see Tuarra. It will make me leave Azorra one way or the other."

I began to understand why the ephelos—the voice—had failed so often before in the men it had lifted off their own planets and to his own. This was a strange, barbaric world where only a fighting man could exist. The voice could take command of my body and my brain but when it did so I was no more than an automaton. It could not fight for me. It could only counsel and advise and make me perform certain actions when I was not in danger. I knew well enough that I would never be able to go back to Tuarra unless I obeyed the voice. First bring the ephelos what it needed, then I would be free to fulfill my own destiny here on Llarn.

I told all this to Ulazza, who sat sobbing with bent head. Finally she nodded and looked at me with wet eyes. "The ephelos chose well in you, Alan Morgan. No one else could have come so far without losing his life."

Her sorrowful eyes told her that I might lose my life in my attempt to escape from Azorra, but that I would surely lose it when I encountered the ephelos. They told me also that she understood I must go on my mission, and that I must go alone. For her to go with me was for her to die.

In her eyes, I was already dead.

She sighed and lifted out the sword and dagger she had smuggled into the cell in her garments, buckling them onto my belt chains with her own hands. Then she threw her arms around my neck and kissed me.

I would have removed her arms, for I was thinking of Tuarra at the moment, but since she felt she was sending me to my death, the least I could do was let her think there was a chance that someday I might return her love.

There is no day and no night in the tunnels of Azorra. Only the lamps made brightness and once they were removed everything was a Stygian darkness. Two of the lamps were inside the cell with us. The third one was outside it, near the bench where a guard sat, half drowsing.

I extinguished the cell lamps as Ulazza lay down to sleep. I waited until the guard was also half asleep before slipping out the cell key and unlocking the barred door. The lock had been well lubricated. It made no sound other than a tiny clink of falling tumblers. Then I was outside the cell and stepping sideways into the gloom of a nearby tunnel.

The guard dozed on. He never suspected that anyone was within reaching distance of him until my fist thudded into his jaw. I bound him with his weapon belt and gagged him, then took the lamp from its wall hook.

With the lamp before me, I moved into the corridor that ran straight for half a mile before it opened into three intersecting tunnels. In my mind, I had the plan of these cellars spread out so that I would make no mistake. Even so, it was a longer process than I planned on.

I must have made a wrong turn, for I found myself in a dead end alleyway which opened onto a great subterranean lake in which phosphorescent creatures moved about. Was this part of the now dry sea of Uzzal, that had lapped the shores of Azorra before The War? Or was it the source of the drinking water that made Azorra still a habitable city? I promised myself that someday I would return to learn the answers.

Right now I was more concerned with finding the chest that held the rod of taliforr. I put the lamp down and unrolled the map of the cellarways. Yes, here I was, and here I had made the wrong turn. I must retrace my steps and take the middle tunnel.

I made good progress after that. When I hesitated I brought out the map and examined it. Soon, I stood over a dusty chest with a rusted lock, wth the temple of Arone above me. Five blows of a daggerhilt shattered the lock and I threw back the lid.

A narrow rod of green metal lay on a large cushion.

The rod of taliforr! Lift it, put it in your belt!

I did as the voice ordered. Then I checked the map once more. I found the one place in all that maze of corridors that would lead me out beyond the walls of Azorra. Where the tunnels showed straight without a turn, I ran at full speed. Where there was intersections I waited, listening for sounds of pursuit. There were none. Apparently I was alone in this corner of underground Azorra.

I came out of the tunnels into darkness. The cold night wind I had felt back in the last tunnel as I walked along told me clearly enough that freedom lay before me. I extinguished my lamp and left it on the dusty floor as I walked out under the stars and the great band of shattered matter that had been the moons of Llarn long, long ago.

I made my way between a row of high bushes and then

through a grove of trees, making a circle about the high walls until I saw my flier lying in plain sight of the wall battlements. I had no way of knowing whether the Azunn maintained a night guard on those walls. I had to assume they did and so I crawled on my belly out to the flier, pausing often to blend myself with the landscape as best I could.

Dawn was a red tint in the sky when I reached the little ship and strapped myself on. I rose above the ground to the height of a few feet and like this, using a stand of trees as a background, I traveled for about a mile.

Then I pushed over the controls and rose into the sky.

No red needle beam showed itself, nor was there any sound from Azorra. I fled southward and westward from the city of the blue men as fast as my propellors could churn.

By mid-morning of the next day I sighted a faint white line all along the horizon. The noon sun found me moving over the southerly icecap of the planet, a great field of snow and ice that extended for uncounted miles. The air was cold. I shivered steadily, for as the flier traveled above that snowy expanse an icy wind blew on me steadily.

Slow down, man of Earth. Slowly, slowly.

I reduced the speed of the little ship until it barely maintained altitude. Off to one side I saw a mighty glasslike bubble thrusting above the ice pack.

Land and enter the dome as I direct.

The metal keel skidded on the ice and brought up against a big snowdrift. I felt for the metal ball and the green rod as I stepped out onto the ice. In only my kilt and weapons belt, with the high sandals that encased my feet, I was scarcely dressed for walking around in the cold. I legged it toward the great dome.

As I drew closer, I saw that the dome itself was of the same transparent substance that the dome of the pink mists had been. There were ebon mists inside this dome, however, and they shifted and moved as if blown by small winds.

In answer to the bidding of the voice, I placed my hands

palm down on a band of purple metal. It felt warm, soothing. There was a pause, then the dome appeared to move, turning upon its base until—

The black mists churned, puffed outward all around me. *The gate has opened. Enter!*

I stepped into the blackness, felt it wrap itself about me as if to warm and comfort my cold flesh. I drew a few breaths, felt the tiredness and the cold seep out of me. Never have I felt so alive as I did at that moment. Whatever was in the blackness had a marvelous affect upon the human body.

The black mists parted, opening a pathway for my feet along a metal floor that led toward an opening in the metal. I walked toward it until I saw a flight of metal steps leading downward into a pale pink radiance.

I went down the stairway, slowly.

My heart was hammering. I had no way of knowing whether I walked to my death, as Ulazza had foretold. As soon as my eyes rested on the ephelos, I might be blasted into nothingness. Or shrivelled to a bag of bonelessness. Or thrust into an agony so intense I might go mad.

Yet I walked down and down.

I must have entered the dome at a great height, which the pink mists mercifully hid. At length a floor of that same pink metal stretched before me. I walked along it where the pink mists parted. The thought came to me that the pink mists protected me in some manner. Perhaps they absorbed the radiation which the ephelos gave off, so that I would be unharmed by it.

Stop! Remove the ball and the rod.

I halted and took them out of my purse. I held them in my hand, waiting.

The pink mists opened a little more. Faintly, faintly I could see a golden ball—a helix—a prism—from which streamed faery tentacles of wire thinness, joined to other, smaller prisms of that same blinding brightness. It quivered and throbbed with a faint tinkling as of many bells. It hovered above the floor, growing always brighter until it drove away the mists near it and hung alone in glittering splendor.

It was like nothing I had ever imagined.

It was alive, sentient. The thought that this thing might once had been a man made the hair rise on the back of my neck. I was rooted to the spot, unable to move a muscle.

So. We see each other at last, face to—face.

I could only nod.

You have done well, Earthman! You are the first of many who have been able to do my bidding. For this metal ball and this green rod are the means by which I may leave this planet of my birth.

The golden helix pulsed as it telepathed its thoughts at me. I heard them as I had always heard the voice. It hung there and spoke to me and made me understand the long centuries of loneliness it had endured from the moment of its change until this moment.

The ephelos had been a human being, once.

Long ago, before The War, he had lived in a city called Loth. He was fifteen years of age when the bombs had fallen on Loth and the radioactive dust had bathed him and his people in its poisons. Only for the young boy who had been Vann Tar it had not been poison but—something else.

There had been pain, yes. And oozing lesions all over his body. He had lain in the wreckage of his home with only his mind alive, for a long time. At first he had been hungry but the hunger had gone away after a time so that he lay in a stupor until he discovered that he had no need to move his body to eat. He could separate himself from his flesh and blood, leaving his body behind and traveling great distances as a disembodied consciousness.

He went out in this astral form and bathed in the radio-activity in his city and fed on it until his astral self glowed red. When he sought to return into what had been his body, he could not. The flesh and bones of his physical body were inert. Their usefulness to him was passed. He was no longer a human being but a radiation-changed intelligence.

He had no idea how long he remained in the ruined ashes of Loth. He fed and fed on that radioactivity until he had swallowed it whole. His astral body had enlarged, grown tentacles and a core of golden radioactive matter. No longer was his substance astral but radioactive energy. With his increase in size and substance came an added intelligence. His brain was sharp, super-normally observant.

During the long weeks, months, years that he remained in Loth his senses quested throughout the city. He could read—and understand—the ancient books of wisdom hidden in the libraries of his city. For lack of anything better to do, he searched what was left of the museums and the public buildings, and added to his growing understanding. He matured and aged.

His parahuman intelligence brooded on what he had learned, discovered new laws of science and how to adapt himself to them. It took a long time. Time was as nothing to him who was timeless, however. He knew he could not age, that he was deathless.

Or so that which had been Vann Tar thought.

When the radioactivity in the city had been absorbed, he moved out and away from it, to where it was still strong. This radioactivity he absorbed too, until he—with perhaps a half dozen others of his kind, all of whom had been formed by the awesome nuclear activity of The War—had rid the planet of its dangerous blight.

The ephelos had learned over the years that he meant death to any human he approached. His core was so filled with radioactivity that he could not prevent its seeping forth to doom his former fellow humans. In time he gathered back that radioactivity inside himself, but by then it was too late.

And so all the epheloin retired to distant places.

They spent their time thinking. It was a mutual thinking together, for the epheloin were telepathic. The thoughts of one were common to them all. And in time they realized they were not immortal. Death could claim them, and it would—unless certain things were done.

There were two substances which were needed by them to be absorbed—at the exact moment when they flowered—which would render them deathless. It would also give them the power to make themselves immune to gravity or to other known forces in the universe. Each had absorbed all the radioactive energies he needed to live on, turning out within his tentacled prisms all the radioactivity he needed for life, refeeding it through the tentacles into the prisms and again absorbing it.

The two new substances were something else.

They must not be absorbed before the exact instant when they were needed to effect the changeover. Therefore they must be made ready against need.

The epheloin learned that these substances, when found by the human beings Llarn, were thought to be very valuable. They were taken away and locked up, sometimes made into jewelry for the womenfolk of the planet, sometimes into crowns for its rulers.

And so the epheloin learned to hide them under glass domes and surrounded by the pink mists or hidden away in dusty chests in the cellars of ancient and forgotten cities.

No Llarnian could fetch these substances to the ephelos in need of them, however. The Llarnian always died before he could deliver his previous cargo. And so the epheloin went hunting. They drew their messengers from distant planets, by teleportation. Always the wrench of that passage was numbing. The ephelos who called on an alien being needed time to recover and—sometimes the alien was killed before he could complete his mission.

The quest took time, but time was meaningless to the epheloin. Over the many centuries since The War, one by one the epheloin—went out. Only he who had been Vann Tar remained.

Now it is my time to go!

The golden prism expanded, grew before my eyes. It filled

107

the underground chambers until its brightness was a torment. My arms were up before my eyes to hide myself from that brilliance. I was positive that the next moment I would be dead.

Fear not, Earthman. I repay kindness with kindness.

Before you came to Llarn, I placed the black mists in the ice dome above. They are a counter to the radiation that fills my core. As you walked into them, the black mists formed a veil upon your flesh. My radiation is harmless to you with that invisible coating.

The warmth bathed me, now. It whispered to me, soothing my muscles, adding new life, new strength to them. I lifted my head. No longer did the brilliance of the ephelos bother me.

I could watch as the great golden helix extended its slim filaments toward the green rod and the red ball. The golden wires hovered above those metallic objects as though savoring this moment of triumph. Then they lowered, gripping the rod and the ball.

The outlines of the rod and ball shimmered. Slowly they lost their shape. The green and the red grew pale, colorless. Then the outlines shimmered . . . quavered . . . and were gone.

The rod and ball existed only inside the golden prism.

In their place something like a great green teardrop glistened on the floor. It looked like an emerald, cold and flawless. It had formed within the helix as the energies of the rod and ball were absorbed, like some priceless byproduct of that awesome fusion.

I bent, lifted the jewel, held it in my palm.

The golden helix pulsed more brilliantly.

I am changing, yes! No longer is my substance Llarnbound. I can slip upwards into space or—sideways into the other dimensions that surround our universe. Into those other universes I can go as you might walk upon the land, man of Earth!

It was a wild, pagan song of victory. It rang in my ears

with ineffable sweetness and delight. The helix shimmered. It too grew pale and colorless, lost its outlines and vanished from my sight.

The pink mists disappeared. The floor and walls of the underground chamber lost their strength and lustre. They too faded away, revealing an uneven surface underfoot scattered with the debris of centuries. Stalagmites rose upward as if from nowhere. Above my head stalactites appeared, dripping with lime and water.

I shivered. Even though the dampness of the cavern was chilling me, my forehead was covered with sweat. I turned and ran.

Fortunately, the spiraling staircase still stood but it was ancient, old, and it creaked when I set foot on it. It swayed and groaned the higher I climbed. Twice I clung to it, fearing it would give way to my weight and plummet me down to an awful death on those jagged stalagmites.

It was an age before I leaped from the top step of the stairway onto the solid metal of the staircase rim. This too was old, old. It powdered where my foot hit it.

Gone were the black mists and the transparent dome that had held them, gone the purple metal. My eyes saw only a vast expanse of ice and snow, and my flier tilted over so that the sunlight glinted on its keel.

I ran for it as if the devil were at my heels.

CHAPTER EIGHT

As I ROSE upward over the snowfields, I had only one thought in my head. At all costs, I must reach Kharthol as fast as possible to prevent the marriage of Tuarra to Gorlun Duv. Nothing else mattered.

The controls were on full before I was ten feet above the ice. The little craft sped upward at a slant, gathering speed at every second. The white surface became a blur below me. I clung to the narrow deck, snapping on the last of my flying harness. My flesh did not mind the cold; it was warm with a sense of desperation that sent me hurtling through the frosty air of this polar zone at breakneck swiftness.

I had no map but only a recollection of the general direction in which I had come. I aimed my sharp prow north by northeast and hung on.

The snowfields gave way to great, barren tundras. The tundras went away before lush grasslands and low hills. The air grew warmer. Overhead the star-sun Alfan was a great globe in the sky.

Dusk shrouded Llarn, a dusk through which I raced like a demented soul. I held the flier to its maximum capacity even though it trembled throughout its length. It might shake itelf apart long before I reached Kharthol, I knew, but I had to take the risk.

I slept fitfully through the night.

The rising sun was a redness in the east as I flew high enough to skin the hills that ran in a rough line north to south across this section of Llarn. Beyond the hills I saw the ruins of a lost and forgotten city. The surface of Llarn is dotted with many such relics of a former world. Always they intrigue me with a sense of mystery and wonder. What hidden treasures lay deep in their vaults? What men and women once walked their streets proudly and with pleasure? I fought down the impulse to land and examine them.

The hunger I felt to see Tuarra, to save her from the tyrant of Kharthol, overrode all my other desires. I turned and looked my last on that towering pile of rock and marble.

Then I was facing ahead, speeding above the grasses and the winds blowing through them. I think I dreamed a little of Tuarra then, seeing her face before me with its golden skin and thick black hair, her red lips and gentle eyes. I wondered how I was to save her.

As I say, I dreamed of her.

I have no other excuse for not seeing the blue men on the striped drals racing along one side of the flier, attempting to cut me off. Their needle-guns were in their hands and with them they were spraying the air around me.

I woke to the sense of danger when the flier lurched. I lifted off my medallion and held it out. A dozen needle-beams were attracted to it, splashing in a sunburst of power as they hit its surface. But I was too late. One of the red rays had ripped a gash in my keel and plowed through part of the motor itself.

The little ship was sinking lower. In a few hundred years, it would hit the ground, perhaps roll over on me. I unsnapped my belt and tensed myself to jump.

Five feet above the ground I leaped. An instant later the ship dug its prow into the soft loam of these grasslands and shuddered. Its propellor wailed a scream into the air before the motor died.

The Azunn were coming for me at the gallop.

I yanked my blade free of its scabbard and waited. There were half a dozen of them and I felt my heart leap. I had faced greater odds than this on Llarn.

To my surprise, they reined up about twenty feet away. One of their number, a lesser chieftain to judge by the number of the white feathers on his saddle, lifted a hand, palm toward me.

"You are Alan Morgan?"

Wondering, I told him I was.

"Morlan Az sends greetings and a pardon. He asks you to accompany us to Azorra. You are to be an honored guest. A friend."

My ears tingled with disbelief. Morlan Az had thrown me in a jail cell and ordered my execution last time I had stood before him. What could have changed his mind about my fate? Certainly not Ulazza, who had shared my cell. I was puzzled and suspicious, but . . .

Every man has hope locked inside his chest. I might kill

these half dozen riders if they attacked me, which they seemed not about to do, or I might not. Even if I killed them all and mounted one of the drals, it was a long ride back to Kharthol through much of the Azunn heartland.

I could not fight the entire nation of blue men.

My sword went back into the scabbard and I advanced on the riders. I was tensed for trouble, but their faces were innocent of guile. One of them shifted in his saddle, urging me up behind him.

When I was firmly planted on the animal's croup, I began to ask questions. I wanted to know why Morlan Az had changed his mind, why he wanted me alive—and my skin crawled. Of course!

It was the right of every Llarn ruler to assess the punishment for a crime, if he so desired. My crime had been against the person of the Azunn dagan. Morlan Az wanted me alive and well, able to withstand the tortures which his brain would dream up.

The young sub-chief vigorously disagreed with this.

"More than a hundred searching parties like ourselves were despatched south of Azorra to hunt for you. We had strict orders not to harm you, and while we were told nothing of what Morlan Az plans, we were given to understand that far from your being in danger, Morlan Az now considers you his friend."

This was more puzzling than ever.

We rode for almost an entire day and part of a night— the young chieftain explained that he was under strict orders to get me to Azorra as fast as possible—stopping only to eat and rest the drals. A little after the middle of the night we trotted into the capital city of the Azunn.

Word of our coming must have preceeded us. The lights were on in the palace as we dismounted in the great square and went up the stone steps. Ulazza was there, waiting for me.

She caught my hands and smiled up into my face. "You are safe, Alan Morgan, in case you have been wondering."

"What changed your brother's mind? What's happened?"

She would not tell me, only walked beside me with the young sub-chief on the other side, across the antechamber and into the brightly lighted throne room. I saw Morlan Az standing beside another, older man—a man with the golden skin of the Vrann—who swung around to face me.

Morlan Az came forward with his hands held high. Ulazza whispered for me to do the same, to touch my palms to his. As I did so, Morlan Az smiled. Now that he was no longer an enemy, I could see him in a new light. He was a handsome man, strong and muscular, with a trace of the beauty which Ulazza possessed in his straight nose and firm mouth, clear eyes and high forehead.

"Welcome to Azorra, Alan Morgan," he said. "No longer are you a foe of the blue men but a valued friend." He swung toward the older man, the Vrann. "Let me present Drakol Tu—the deposed dagan of Kharthol."

"You must be Tuarra's father," I exclaimed.

Drakol Tu laughed with resonance in his deep voice. "Yes," he told me as we touched palms. "I have already been told that you took her safely out of Azorra—how, nobody knows."

I explained how I had met the khorl, Kav Mork, and how he teleported Tuarra and me out of Azorra to the seaport city of Krondys. Their faces whitened at my tale, for Llarnians fear the khorls amost as they do the epheloin. As I spoke, Ulazza guided me and the others to another room where a table had been piled with food and drink.

Morlan Az growled when I explained how I had fought the mind-beast created by the khorl, and Drakol Tu sat shaken when I told of the trick Kav Mork played on me, and of my despair at discovering he had fled with Tuarra while leaving me to my fate on the empty island of Inislan.

Only Ulazza sat silent, but her eyes glowed when I related how I found the flier and embarked on it for distant Kharthol. She was very close to me, and from time to time would put her hand on my forearm. Whenever I paused in my narration, she took it upon herself to feed me bits of meat from the platters.

Morlan Az and Drakol Tu exclaimed as I told how I had come back to Azorra for the green rod, and how my mission summoned me to stand face to face with an ephelos. Their eyes were wide as they leaned forward to hear my every word, as I made them see an ephelos in their mind, the first time anyone on Llarn had heard a description of one. No one who had seen an ephelos before now had returned to tell about it.

Drakol Tu smiled faintly. "Had we known that the aliens who came to Llarn from time to time were here to rid us of those creatures, we would not have interfered with them."

Morlan Az nodded, frowning. "Sometimes a man does not know his friends and—his enemies—until it is too late."

The dagan of the Azunn glanced at me. "Know, man of Earth, that Drakol Tu who was my foe is now my ally. As are you, if you will join us."

I had finished my story. I asked them to explain what had happened while I had been south in the icelands of Llarn.

Morlan Az said slowly, heavily, "As you may know, I made alliance with Gorlun Duv some time ago. When he rebelled against Drakol Tu, I was to act as jailer to the deposed dagan who was turned over to us. At the same time, I was to hold Tuarra my prisoner—also threatening her father with death unless she consented to wed with Gorlun Duv."

Tuarra had escaped, met up with me, and had been brought to Azorra. Morlan Az had informed the new dagan of Kharthol that the princess of Kharthol was safely in his hands. Before Tuarra could be sent on to marry him, however, she escaped with me from Azorra.

Kav Mork had done his work for him, Morlan Az added heavily, so that now Gorlun Duv refused to pay the price the Azunn ruler had asked for his alliance. Kharthol was to have entered into a trade agreement with the blue people, to give and accept the palm of friendship.

Now Gorlun Duv had repudiated his promises.

"What could I do? My main concern is always with my people, what is best for them. Trade with Kharthol would open up more cities of the Vrann to us. All that was a mad dream, unless I could form a new alliance."

Morlan Az went on, "I turned to the true ruler of Kharthol. I asked Drakol Tu if he would do what Gorlun Duv had promised to do and would not."

"I was happy to agree," Drakol Tu said. "For a long while, I have thought that trade with the Azunn would spur our own economy, help my people as it would help the Azunn." He smiled ruefully. "I am afraid Morlan Az may be wasting his strength on me, however. I am no longer strong in Kharthol. I am nothing."

Long imprisonment had eaten at his pride. I hastened to reassure him, to explain that all Kharthol fretted under Gorlun Duv. I related what Barrluk Tann had told me, that only his personal army units kept the usurper on the throne. All Kharthol needed was a leader around whom to rally.

"You shall be that leader, Drakol Tu," I assured him. "Lift up your banner. Free Khartholians will gather around it. Gorlun Duv will have only his own army units to fight you. And even some of those will come over to us, I am sure."

Morlan Az and Drakol Tu looked at one another, their faces heavy with despair. Ulazza sat quietly, her hand on mine.

The silence deepened. It was Ulazza who answered my unspoken query as I looked from one face to another. "The princess Tuarra is bethrothed to Gorlun Duv. Once she weds him, Gorlun Duv will have a legal claim to the throne. Then the only way Drakol Tu could hope to take back his throne would be by a hand to hand conflict in which he killed the dagan."

Drakol Tu shrugged. "I am an older man. Gorlun Duv is

in the prime of manhood. Besides, he is the greatest warrior in Kharthol. He has never known the taste of defeat."

I rose to walk around the room. My eyes touched a heavy wall drapery, the metal of a statue, the bowl of copper hanging from the ceiling beams in which a thin plume of perfumed incense rose in the air currents. My thoughts were on none of them, but on Tuarra.

I saw her face in front of me, felt the touch of her lips in a phantom kiss. I held her in my arms in my imagination and—I knew that life without her would be no life. I knew also that I could save his throne for Drakol Tu.

"I will go alone to Kharthol while you gather your warriors," I said slowly. "I made a good friend there who will be wondering what has become of me. I will go to him, enlist his aid—and get the princess out of Kharthol."

Ulazza stirred, almost angrily. Morlan Az glanced from his sister to me with a little smile upon his lips. The dagan of Kharthol—in my mind he was still its ruler—sat looking at me intently.

"How can one man bring my daughter out of Kharthol?"

My forefinger tapped the hilt of my sword. Drakol Tu expelled a sigh and leaned back, frowning at me. "No one man can fight all of Kharthol," he said heavily, as though accusing me of boastfulness.

Ulazza laughed. "You have not seen Alan Morgan fight, highness. His will not be a suicide mission."

I assured Drakol Tu that I did not mean to take on the entire Khartholian military might. One man could enter Kharthol, contact the daganna, slip with her from the city. Though Drakol Tu shook his head gloomily, foreseeing only death for me and disaster to his hopes, he could think of no other solution.

"Once Gorlun Duv weds Tuarra, he will rule in Kharthol. I will be the Pretender to the throne, then. Yes, first Tuarra must be set free—for were we to attack while he has her in his power, he would immediately force her to marry him."

So it was arranged. I went with Drakol Tu and Morlan

116

Az to a small armory where a film of golden paste was worked into my flesh, tinting it the proper color so that I might pass for a golden Vrann. When the masseurs were done. I was as much a Vrann as was Drakol Tu himself.

Then we went to a different part of the city, where I had never been before. Behind a high wall, the dagan of Azorra had hidden half a dozen fliers. At my look of astonishment, he chuckled.

"The Azunn do not fly, but from time to time we manage to capture a flier belonging to the goldskins." His hand gestured. "Take you pick, Alan Morgan."

They rested on their keels before me, sleek cruisers and small craft, each fashioned so skillfully that they gave the impression of speed even upon the ground. I wanted a small ship, not a big one; I turned to Drakol Tu for help.

"I know swordsmanship, highness," I explained, "but where it comes to fliers, I'll defer to your greater wisdom. You select the ship."

Drakol Tu looked pleased. He believed me to be a boastful adventurer, I am sure, and had not the circumstances of a strange fate linked our fortunes he would have had nothing to do with me. When I asked his advice, he was taken back at first, then nodded slowly, giving me a long look.

"There is a Khartholian ship here, a very new one, faster and more maneuverable than any before it. It was an experimental ship. We never did learn what happened to Avral Kol, its pilot."

Morlan Az said with a shrug of his shoulders, "A patrol found the ship down near the ruins of Kosteran. There was no pilot anywhere in sight."

For over three kors the dagan of Kharthol explained the control of the flier to me. This craft would travel at speeds of better than two thousand erns an hour. It had a retracting plasticine dome that slid up and over the pilot to protect him from the air current. It was a bullet with a motor.

On this flier I could be in Kharthol in less than ten kors. I felt excitement run along my veins. I was that close to

Tuarra! Almost instantly, the excitement was followed by something akin to despair. Was she wedded with Gorlun Duv? Had she in her own despondency when I failed to appear, leaped from a high battlement or driven a dagger into her heart? My hands were shaking in sudden terror. I had to fit them over the flier controls to still them.

Drakol Tu had been watching emotion wash across my features. He put his heavy hand on my shoulder. His eyes were more friendly than they had been.

"If any man on Llarn can save her, Alan Morgan," he murmured, "you can." It was a vote of confidence I badly needed at the moment. He hesitated, then added, "I have not mentioned this before but if Gorlun Duv does wed Tuarra, there is yet a way by which you can win her, if you are the swordsman Ulazza claims you to be."

An old law of Llarn stated that if a man could kill another in hand to hand combat, his wife belonged to the victor if he wanted her. It was all but forgotten, but it was still a law. If I should find Gorlun Duv married to Tuarra, I could challenge the dagan to mortal combat. Frowning, I pointed out that I was no true Khartholian and that might make a difference.

Drakol Tu shook his head, admitting he did not know about this legal point, though he felt reasonably certain it would still apply. He asked how I planned to enter Kharthol.

I told him I intended arriving at the cattle holdings of Barrluk Tann sometime after dark, where I would explain to Barrluk Tann what had happened. I would ask his help in organizing an armed revolt against Gorlun Duv. While Barrluk Tann was gathering a volunteer force, Darkol Tu would be doing the same on the farflung frontier world of Kharthol.

"Once I have Tuarra out of Kharthol, I'll give Barrluk Tann the signal. You and he will be in touch by that time. Then you can both mount your attacks."

It was as good a plan as any, he agreed glumly. Drakol Tu was not an optimist.

I wanted to waste no more time. I slid onto the flier, buckled on my flying harness, revved the motor. With Ulazza and her brother and Drakol Tu watching, I lifted the flier, circled it twice in a salute, then turned its metal prow to Karthol.

I could feel the difference between this sleek masterpiece and the ancient ship that had taken me off the isle of Inislan. In Earth terms, the old crate had been a World War One Jenny, and this was an A-11. It fled through the sky like a lightning bolt.

By nightfall I was less than a hundred erns from Kharthol. I slowed my speed and made a great circle to avoid the patrol boats that fly back and forth on the edge of all Llarnian cities as protection against sudden attack.

By the brilliance of the great matter ring overhead I could pick out the farm buildings that belonged to Barrluk Tann. He had described them well enough so that I knew them at sight. I landed after a long glide with my motors stilled and left the ship under a killosa bush.

Barrluk Tann himself opened the door to my knock. His eyes grew wide and round at sight of me. He reached out and dragged me inside.

"I never thought to see you again, man! When you didn't appear before the princess, I sent word to her by my sister, who is working on her wedding dress, that—"

"Tuarra isn't married yet?" I asked breathlessly.

"Not yet, no. You've been gone less than a trod. The marriage is planned for next trod plus one."

Barrluk Tann explained how he had gotten word to Tuarra that I had had a metal ball on my person, that it was because of that elathin I had come to Llarn in the first place. He knew nothing about the ephelos because at the time I had shown him the metal ball, I knew nothing of it myself, other than the fact that a voice had spoken to me.

"She thinks you're dead," he told me now.

"Then I have to relieve her mind."

I would have walked right out of the spacious farmhouse

119

except that Barrluk Tann dissuaded me. "Wait, wait," he laughed. "You can't rush into Kharthol and out again with the daganna as a thief might run from a house with a rare jewel."

"Why not?" Where Tuarra was concerned, I could do anything I put my mind to, I told him.

"Maybe, maybe. But listen to sense. Let me at least get word to my sister, and plan another meeting for you with Tuarra. If you were to wander all over the palace looking for her, you'd be spotted in no time."

His words cooled my ardor. Grudgingly I admitted that his way might be better than mine. I followed him down into the bowels of his farmhouse, and found it a far more spacious place than it seemed from the air. I was to learn that on Llarn, all houses outside the city limits were built mostly beneath the ground. All that showed on the surface were a few buildings.

The War had taught the Llarnians to be ready for another holocaust. As a result, their homes were their nuclear shelters. Here in comparative safety they could indulge their tastes for the beautiful and the exotic, with hanging of costly brocade, with painted masterpieces on the walls and illumined by hidden lights, with glass walls and smartly tiled floors. I saw bright scarlet blossoms and purple petals and the rich cream of many flowers.

The furniture was low and wide, and very comfortable.

Barrluk Tann touched a button on a wall panel and the air filled with music. From a wooden upright he lifted tall glasses filled with a rich, soothing liquid.

As I sipped, I complimented him on his home.

"It has been the home of my ancestors for centuries," he answered. "These paintings, the statuary, are very old, very precious. I add to them when I am able, from current profits. The collection was begun some years after The War by an early ancestor. We who follow him take pride in making it the finest outside the city limits."

He crossed the room and pulled back a drape, revealing

120

a glass screen inset in metal. As he turned dials the screen came alive, fuzzy and distorted. Slowly it cleared until I saw the interior of another room, a living room of some sort, filled with the same massive furniture as that in the room where I sat. A woman came into view, small and pretty. Her resemblance to Barrluk Tann was quite obvious.

They conversed in low tones for a little while, then Barrluk Tann explained that he was sending her a new employee to be fitted for the regulation uniform worn by the cattle herders of his farm. As he spoke I watched his right hand move, its fingers sliding back and forth.

Barrluk Tann murmured a farewell, was answered in the same manner. He turned to me and grinned. "Gorlun Duv had monitored many of the vocal viewers," he told me. "He has paid spies listening to the conversations among the people, to uncover plots against him. My sister and I worked out a system of signals. Crude but effective. She knows you are more than an employee and has agreed to help."

I would leave for Kharthol in the morning. I would go to the shop of Alta Tann and be outfitted as a cattle herder. This would serve as an excuse to take up lodgings in Kharthol. While my uniform was being made, Alta Tann would get word to Tuarra that I was in Kharthol, and set up a meeting between us.

"After that, you're on your own," Barrluk Tann said.

"Not quite," I grinned back at him.

I told him of Drakol Tu, of the army that the Azunn were forming to help the real dagan of Kharthol get back his throne. I told my friend that his ruler had asked for his help to recruit troops on the grasslands. I explained that once Tuarra was safe, the attack would begin.

Barrluk Tann sat down and leaned back in a chair. "It has come. I knew it would, some day—if Drakol Tu still lived. I and others like me have made certain preparations. We have gathered weapons, hired former soldiers, veterans of old Kartholian wars."

When he saw my surprise, he chuckled. "I have more than

two thousand men on my payroll right now who are ready and eager to take up arms. So have my neighbors. I know of camps far to the east where men are waiting patiently for word to attack the usurper."

His eyes fixed me with a stare. "We need a leader. We are ready to strike fast and hard, but we need a man to follow, to give orders. You will be that leader, Alan Morgan—if you can rescue Tuarra."

He swallowed the last of his drink. "Now you will sleep while I make arrangements to arm and equip those troops, and have them ready for the attack."

I had not thought I was tired, but when Barrluk Tann led me to a room adjoining the great living quarters, I collapsed on the big round bed. I slept like a dead man, and did not wake until Barrluk Tann himself stood beside the bed, shaking my shoulders.

I had slept the clock around and then again a halfnight. It was a little after dawn. A dral was being saddled for me in the big courtyard on the surface.

"You will leave the dral at a road stable an ern from Kharthol," he told me. "Within the city proper, drals are not permitted. You must proceed on foot. I'll make sure you have plenty of money, so you won't want for anything. Come, dress yourself and eat."

By mid-morning I was well on my way toward Kharthol, which I could see as a distant haze on the horizon. A flier was infinitely faster than this striped dral but the dral was a good animal, strong and fleet. I overtook and passed many other riders and quite a few family wagons.

Barrluk Tann had given me a plasticine pass, the kind issued to all his men. It bore my name and signature and a series of numbers that would tell something of my past. The numbers were a lie, of course, but by the time they were checked out, I would have Tuarra out of Kharthol or be dead.

I left the dral at the road stable.

I joined the other walkers to and from the great city.

122

The guards at the gate merely glanced at my pass before gesturing me on into the city. Barrluk Tann had given me a map of Kharthol to memorize. I found that I had done my work well; my feet paced its streets and alleys as though used to them all my life.

I went to the same public house where Barrluk Tann and I had stayed before. Nothing was changed. There were even one or two familiar faces among them. I arranged to have my sleeping silks ready upon my return, and set out for the shop of Alta Tann.

I walked by way of the street that wound past the palace gardens, where I had walked the night when the ephelos had come to claim me for the mission on which it had brought me to Llarn. It was here the ephelos had whispered to me, roused from its torpidity after lifting me off Earth.

Then, I had been on my way to find Tuarra. Now I was hoping for a glimpse of her as I kept glancing at the palace walls. For the most part, those stone walls were thick and impenetrable, but here and there round openings were fitted—moon windows—through which a passerby might catch a glimpse of the riotous blossoms of the royal gardens.

I stood a little while before one of the openings until the curious looks of the passersby told me no Khartholian in his right mind would stand there so long. I moved on. Then, at the last window, I saw Tuarra.

She was moving across a terrace high up on the palace. She wore the royal black and gold kiltlike skirt below the harness about her slim middle. A bolero of matching gauze held her shoulders and breasts. Her thick black hair was piled high and set with jeweled combs. She was pagan, barbaric, and—the lovelist woman on two worlds.

I almost shouted to her. I came close to clambering through the moon window and running across the gardens to take her in my arms. If I had needed anything to make me more determined to rescue her, it was the momentary sight of my princess moving across the terrace. Her head hung down a little, as if she were intolerably sad.

I waited there until she passed from view, not caring how many looks I got, not caring about anything but Tuarra of Kharthol. At last, when she was gone, I turned and all but ran to the shop of Alta Tann.

She was waiting for me. She conducted me to her inner office where she sat down and studied me. After a little time, she nodded.

"Yes, you may be able to do it. I thought at first my brother was mad when I understood what it was he wanted of me. Now, I'm not so sure." She smiled a little, wryly. "Oh, I've heard the princess speak of you. Always she claims you are the one man who can save her from Gorlun Duv. Until now, I thought she too might be a little mad."

My eyebrows were arched. "You can tell all this from a mere look at me? Just from seeing me?"

She flushed and bit her lip. "There are some of us who are still affected by The War. I possess a sense of—awareness. After being with a person for a little while I seem to feel his or her character. You are a fighting man, Alan Morgan. Odds do not distress you. They only make you fight the better. And the daganna was right. You are a great swordsman."

She clapped her hands. "Enough of this. You must be outfitted. Yes, we will keep up the pretense. But tonight, at the hour of the dral, you are to be at the first moon window nearest the Square of Rulers. You will carry a small bag in which are spare garments for the princess."

I played out the little act, getting measured, studying the uniform which was worn by the herders in the employ of Barrluk Tann. Such a uniform would be made for me and my measurements kept on file, just in case of an investigation by Gorlun Duv.

When I left the shop I carried a small bag in which were stored the garments my princess would wear when she and I fled out of Kharthol. The hour of the dral would be a long time coming. My blood was on fire for some action. I paced the streets of Kharthol a long time, studying the ancient, massive buildings that had withstood the scars of The War, and moved along the fringe of the newer city, rebuilt long after that event.

In the geometrical center of the city was a mighty building that supported the landing flats for the great Khartholian air fleet. It was heavily guarded. Only those who wore the horn insignia of Kharthol on their harness belts were allowed in it. I saw huge fliers rising upward on their eternal patrol of the grasslands that stretched for thousands of erns all around the city, and of the series of irrigation canals that kept them always filled with herbage. On that grass depended much of the economy of Kharthol. A drought would be ruinous. The air fleet defended against attacks on the canals and warned of possible brush fires that might spread.

I ate my evening meal in a little shop not far from the palace. I can never remember what I ate that night; my mind was too filled with the coming hours. Soon I would hold Tuarra in my arms. Soon she and I would be fleeing from Kharthol to my hidden flier. Soon I would be kissing her. Food was tasteless before that expectation.

The hour of the dral succeeds the hour of the bork. Perhaps that single hour was the longest of them all. I could not go out onto the streets and loiter so close to the palace without attracting attention, so I dissembled in the public house, eating and sipping slowly, studying my fellow diners.

I sat there for an eternity.

Then it was time to go. I paid my bill and with my carry-all in hand moved along the cobbled streets of Kharthol toward the first moon window nearest the Square of Rulers. I walked firmly, not too swiftly, yet not slowly. A chronometer which Alta Tann had fastened on my left wrist showed the figure of a horned bork slowly fading into the striped form of a dral.

The moon window was at my elbow.

One glance I threw ahead and one behind me. Nobody was looking in my direction. I leaped upward, gaining the moon window without difficulty. I believe I have said that the gravity of Llarn is not quite that of Earth, so that my muscles are gifted with an added agility that enables me to achieve distances in leaping and speeds in running that would make me something of a superman back on my native planet. I was through the window and into the gardens in one smooth jump.

The gardens were empty save for the great blooms and myself. High overhead the band of crushed moons formed a silver halo of reflected sunlight, beaming it down onto the planet. The gardens were very bright at this time of night. If Tuarra had been here, I would have seen her.

My blood ran cold. She was a prisoner! Gorlun Duv had tumbled to our little scheme. Alta Tann had confessed under torture!

A hand touched my shoulder.

CHAPTER NINE

MY BLADE was half out of my scabbard as I leaped backward half a dozen feet and whirled. I do not know what I expected to see. A dozen armed men, perhaps, ready to fall on me with naked blades.

Instead, I found myself staring at Tuarra of Kharthol.

She was radiantly lovely in a gold and black kilt. Her white leather harness was hung with ebony ornaments, and a tiny bolero of some glittering stuff made her seem surrounded by tiny stars. Above all this was her elfin face, her full red mouth and slanted dark eyes.

I stood and stared at her beauty.

She must have sensed how I felt, for her impishness came to the surface. She posed a little, hand on hip, delighting in my silent admiration. Then her lips parted in a smile and she held out her hands.

I closed the distance between us in one long step and then she was in my arms. I covered her lips with kisses. I whispered of my love to her, of how much she meant to me, of my undying homage to her as a woman. I suppose millions of lovers on every planet from Llarn to Earth have said much the same sort of thing to one another, but to Tuarra and me they were all spanking new.

We kissed, we caressed one another, drawing back to stare deep into each other's eyes. It was foolish to stand here like this in the royal gardens where we might be seen but I had no thought for anything but this woman I loved.

At last, however, she stirred and said softly, "I could stand here forever with you, Alan Morgan, but soon now the guards will make their rounds and—"

I cursed my own stupidity and yanked open the carryall, handing it to her. She seemed to know what to do; Alta Tann had briefed her well. Within seconds she was unfastening her white leather harness straps, dropping them.

"The moon-band is very bright tonight," she said softly.

"The moon-band . . .? Oh!"

I turned my back and stared up at the great band of broken matter, whistling soundlessly while my ears caught the rustle and swish of garments being removed and drawn on, the faint clank where a dagger scabbard rattled its chains. All women on Llarn carry daggers against theft; even a princess was no exception.

"All right, Alan," she said.

She wore simple clothing, now, a beige kilt and worn leather harness, a brown bolero patched in several places. She had removed the jeweled combs from her hair, which she wore long, so that it dangled almost to her hips. The rings on her fingers, her bracelet and earrings, she had wrapped in her discarded clothing, pushing it all under the big roots of a bayanal tree.

I caught her elbow and drew her toward the moon window. I hoisted her up and through, and then came after her. We stood on an empty street.

There was no sound from the gardens, and only distant music from the palace itself. Tuarra laughed softly and slipped her hand into my fingers.

This was the first time we had ever been free and alone on Llarn. Always before, we had been prisoners or Kav Mork had been our companion. We walked swiftly under the silver radiance of the moon shards, to all eyes seemingly no more than a man and his mate strolling homeward.

"Should I take you to my public house?" I asked her. "Or should we make an attempt to pass the gate guards?"

She glanced at me out of the corner of her eyes. "No man takes the woman he loves to a public house," she explained sweetly. "Only one sort of woman goes there."

I flushed and stammered, pleading ignorance of Khartholian customs. Her laughter at my embarrassment was infectious.

"And yet," she went on, head tilted a little to look sideways at me, "it might be the best and safest thing to do. Even Gorlun Duv's guards would never search for me there."

"No," I said firmly, "we'll make a run at the gate."

"That would be madness!" she gasped.

We walked as we spoke, as though we knew just where we were headed. Once or twice a patrol boat moved about us, casting a long shadow in the street. The patrol boats scan the streets as well as the skies, for while the threat of attack by air is almost nonexistent in a time of peace, there are many thieves about their business in the city itself. Should a patrol boat sight suspicious characters, it would sound an alarm and within moments a dozen fliers would be dropping men overside to investigate the disturbance.

"The gate," I said firmly.

"The public house," she announced.

We came close to quarreling, I think. Now that I knew her customs I would have died before subjecting her to the insult of taking her to my sleeping silks. I was learning that

Tuarra had a very practical mind, however; the indignity of an affront to her reputation was far less serious than a threat to her life and mine.

"You are very dear to me, Alan Morgan," she murmured, moving closer so that I could slip an arm about her slender waist. "The gates of Kharthol are heavily guarded. A dozen men, let alone one, could not force them in the dead of night."

"One man might have a chance, were he resourceful," I growled.

"Tomorrow at noon when the crush is greatest, we will leave Kharthol," she declared.

"There is another solution," I said slowly. "Were you to marry me there would be some protection for you if we were caught. It would be for your own safety and the good of Kharthol."

I let my voice trail off as I saw the anger that touched her face. Roughly Tuarra drew away from me, her features cold and haughty. Never had she seemed so much the princess.

"I would not marry you if you were the ruler of all Llarn," she informed me. "I would rather wed a dral!"

Of some such stuff are most lovers' quarrels started. Ours was no exception. I halted on the walkway and caught her by the elbow, swinging her toward me.

"Look, your royal highness! In a sense your father gave me the idea from something he said, just before I left Azorra."

"I don't care if it came from—what was that?"

I told her about meeting her father and that Morlan Az was now his ally. She seemed dazed.

"Alta Tann told me something—I was too excited to pay much attention, I suppose. Besides, we were surrounded by palace serving women in Gorlun Duv's insignia. Go on, go on! Tell me more about my father. Is he well?"

I talked for five minutes, explaining how I had gone with the metal ball and the rod to the ephelos, and how I had been brought to Azorra. Midway in my talk I urged her to walk again, but she maintained her distance from me. For some reason, I had become repulsive to her.

Even as I told her of my experiences in Azorra, I reflected that she had not become insulted by my suggesting she share my sleeping silks, but for some other, to me unknown, reason.

She was silent for such a long time after I finished speaking that I shook her elbow to rouse her from her thoughts. She glanced at me scornfully, chin held high.

"If it is my father's wish, I shall marry you."

"Oh, you idiot," I breathed.

She aimed a slap at my face, but I caught her wrist and drew her against me, holding her helpless with my greater strength as I kissed her. She fought like a cat but I crushed her to me until her struggles ceased. I knew now why she had heaped scorn on me.

"Do you think I love where and when I am ordered to love?" I asked her harshly. "That I need advice from someone else about the woman who is dearer to me than my own life?"

She still panted from exhaustion, but she had lost her scorn. "You said my father—"

"He spoke to me about you only when he realized that I loved you and that I intended to make you mine if I had to fight all Llarn to do it."

She relaxed a little more, even seemed to snuggle closer. In a small voice she complained, "You're hurting me."

I kept my grip on her as I went on. "Only after I had told him how much I loved you did he explain a custom of your people. And he told me that custom, not to influence me to marry you, but that I might turn our marriage to his and your advantage!"

Suddenly she was very meek. "I'm sorry, Alan Morgan. I—I didn't understand. I thought you were marrying me because my father wanted it, that our marriage was to be only a marriage of—convenience."

I wanted to shake her. Could she really believe this of

me? Did not her instincts tell her how much I adored her? I sighed. I had never had much to do with women on my native Earth. The voice had not prepared me to fall in love.

"Come on," I growled, bringing her along beside me at a little run. I was angry, but angry only at myself, at my inability to convince her that I meant what I said about loving her for herself alone.

She trotted for a little way in silence.

Then: "Alan, there is a small temple on a nearby street that is always open, day and night for the convenience of— lovers."

"What do we want with a temple?"

Tuarra sighed. "I keep forgetting you know nothing of our customs. The temple is dedicated to Astarra, who is goddess of love on Llarn. Not that we believe in such things," she added hastily, "but long, long ago when the planet was young, the gods were believed in and—well, the temple is a carryover of the old ways."

We walked a little more.

"The priests of Astarra perform marriages in the temple," she murmured weakly.

With a shout of joy I swung her up into my arms and while she wriggled protestingly, assuring me that a patrol boat would drop down to question us, I ran with her all the way to the little temple. It was a small white building set in a great square, with many pillars all around it and a marble friezework forming its pediment.

"You're sure you want to marry me?" I asked.

Maybe she sensed my own personal hurt, my bitterness. At any rate, she laughed softly and lay against me, kissing my throat. "You are the idiot now, Alan Morgan. I knew you loved me when you caught me in your arms as I tumbled out of that flier in Paloranis."

I was bewildered. "If you know so much, why did you carry on when—"

Her fingertips traced my lips. "A girl likes to be told she

131

is loved for herself, not because marriage with her might save Kharthol for her father."

Women! I could fight my way across a world, then become the most abject fool where Tuarra was concerned. Her fingers hunted along my ribs.

"I would want you no other way," she smiled, as if she could read my mind. Her warm hand caught my fingers and drew me with her into the temple.

The interior was dimly lighted with strips of the glowing metal chemically treated to give off a blue glow. Statues of men and women adorned the wall niches, and tiny altars before them burned fragrant incense. Across many of those altars lay white veils: the marriage veils of women who had offered them up to the goddess.

Tuarra pulled a brocade rope. Faintly from somewhere sounded a myriad tinkling bells. We stood close together in the blueness, waiting.

An old man clad in white approached from the shadows. His eyes widened at sight of Tuarra, then turned to study me.

"Who wishes to wed before Astarra?" he asked.

"The princess Tuarra and the Earthman, Alan Morgan."

I did not protest her use of our true names. Perhaps it was demanded by the rites of the goddess. I only tightened my hand on hers and moved a step closer. The priest smiled faintly, nodding.

"Follow me," he said.

We were conducted into a sanctuary where stood an altar of pure white gorst, an alabaster-like substance exceedingly rare on Llarn. This altar was the largest of its kind on the planet and worth a fortune. All about it were golden tripods holding blossoms floating in holy oil. The priest lifted a small mallet and hit a standing gong.

For most marriages, the outer chamber was filled with guests. The jeweled curtains that hid the altar of Astarra now were drawn back and tied that the guests might see the ceremony, but only two witnesses were to watch as Tuarra

132

and I were wed, another priest and a priestess who stood in a low doorway to the right of the altar.

The priest anointed us with the holy oils, murmured a few words, then asked for the thon. My face was blank, but Tuarra made me understand that the thon was the jewel given by the groom to his bride, somewhat in the same manner that a man slips a wedding band on his wife's finger during an Earth ceremony.

I had no jewel! I had nothing of value outside a few coins Drakol Tu had slipped into my pouch. No, wait! There was something else. When the ephelos had drawn in the metal rod and the ball, a single drop of green hardness had fallen from its flaming core.

I fumbled in my pouch, brought it out.

The priest hissed in his throat when he saw it, and his hand shook. The green jewel appeared to blaze as it caught the dim blue lights, to blaze and glow brightly as if with inner flames.

Tuarra too was staring at it with wide eyes. The witnesses, the priest and priestess, came closer. I could see questions trembling on the lips of the old priest but he did not break the steady rhythm of his chant. He blessed the jewel, and handed it to Tuarra. Her hands closed over it, trembling.

The chant went on.

We were alone, suddenly. The celebrant with the lesser priest and priestess had gone, leaving us by ourselves. I took my princess in my arms and kissed her.

Now that we were husband and wife, we still had to get out of Kharthol. It was imperative that we leave the temple, in case other young lovers should come in after us.

As we walked out, I commented on her rashness in giving her true name to the priest. She told me it would have been no true marriage, and that anything that took place in a temple dedicated to Astarra was sacred all over Llarn. No word of what took place in there, other than the fact that the marriage itself had been celebrated, ever left its walls on pain of a horrible death.

We were safe enough in that direction, at least.

Tuarra lifted out the green jewel, holding it on her palm. "And this? Where did you get this verdal?"

"From the ephelos, as it absorbed the rod and ball."

"There is such a stone, though not as large, in the crown of Kharthol," Tuarra said as we left the temple. "Another is rumored to be in the treasure house of Mornn. Outside of this, those are the only two verdals known to exist."

She asked me to describe to her what had happened, pointing out that I was the only person known to have seen the formation of a verdal. If ever her father ascended to the throne again in Kharthol, she promised she would order an investigation to ascertain how the verdal came to be.

At the moment, however, what concerned us more than any gem was our escape from Kharthol. Tuarra could return with me to the public place now as my wife, but a new thought had come to me.

"Tomorrow the gates may be barred against anyone leaving Kharthol until the disappearance of its future queen is explained to Gorlun Duv's satisfaction," I told her. "Even now, his guards must be searching the palace frantically for you. Gorlun Duv will be like a maniac."

Tuarra admitted ruefully that there was truth to what I said. She understood even better than I how important a marriage to her was to the usurper. When I marvelled that he had not already wedded her, Tuarra laughed.

"I told him I would put a dagger in my ribs if he did not give me time to make up my mind. Gorlun Duv would rather have an acquiescent bride than a corpse. He promised to wait."

"He won't wait any longer—if he catches us."

One glance at her troubled face determined me. My arm still about her middle, I guided her toward the massive gateway. She went willingly enough, but she told me of her concern in little, broken sentences.

"Alan, it is madness. Of the worst sort! There can be

134

only death. For both of us, my darling, when the soldiers see us. I hope it comes swiftly, this death."

"Act," I whispered fiercely. "Pretend with me!"

When we were within the gateway shadows, I swung her to me and kissed her. Tuarra caught on at once, and kissed back as might a public woman with the man who had bought her services. Within seconds a guard was at our elbows.

"Here now," he growled. "Move away. Haven't you any sense at all, man?" As his eyes touched the princess, he saw only an attractive female and grinned. "Well, maybe I can't blame you, but you've got to—"

His words ended in a gasp as my fist sank into his middle, knocking the wind from his lungs. As he doubled up I chopped at his neck with the edge of my hand. He collapsed and lay unmoving.

I dragged him into the shadows where I exchanged my garments for his. Disguised as a guard, I moved into the moonband light and took up my post. In a little while— Tuarra knew to the minute when it would be—a replacement came to stand beside me.

I turned to him, using the hilt of my dagger for added emphasis as I brought my fist up to his jaw. He sank without a sound. I left him in the shadows, tied and trussed and gagged beside his inert companion. Tuarra put on his kilt and harness and swung his cloak about her shoulders.

As guards, we moved toward the little shed housing the machinery which opened the gate. A man dozed inside it. I hit him as Tuarra flashed past me and began working the levers to activate the huge gates.

Luckily, the hinges were heavily oiled. They made no sound as the gates began to open.

We did not wait for their full expanse. Two feet clearance was all we needed. We darted through and ran. At any moment I expected to hear a hail, but the city slumbered at our back.

We avoided the road stretching south across the grasslands, for we would be too visible on its broad surface and even lazy guards might be suspicious of a man and woman running from the city. Our feet sought the rougher portions of the surrounding countryside, where bayanal trees and sinthus bushes grew in great profusion.

Using those shrubs as a background for our running bodies, we fled away from Kharthol. It had been ridiculously simple, as I told my princess.

"You, Alan Morgan," Tuarra panted as we halted to rest. "You always make the impossible seem simple. How you do it, I do not know, but it is a trait I admire very much in you—especially at this moment."

The moon debris high overhead touched her patrician features with cold silver. Her lips were a little parted to aid her breathing. Her heavy black hair was tumbled about her shoulders and down her back. They do not cut women's hair on Llarn, much to my delight, since to my way of thinking her hair is one of a woman's real glories.

I cupped her face in my hands, and kissed her.

"Mrs. Morgan," I laughed softly, and hugged her.

I told her that a married woman on my native planet bore this title. She puzzled over it, frowning slightly. It was strange to her for on Llarn, Tuarra would remain just Tuarra, no matter how many times she married, never taking any of the names of her husbands.

She decided that she liked it, and kissed me with such fervor that I almost forgot we were still within field-glass range of Kharthol. Reluctantly I pushed her away.

"Hurry," I told her.

Once again we ran, but now we went more slowly, for the need of speed was gone. Kharthol slept behind us. Our flier lay ahead. I supported Tuarra for the last few hundred yards with an arm about her waist.

The flier was a small one, not built to hold two people. It rose slowly, lazily, responding sluggishly to my hand on the controls. At a height of fifty feet we circled west of Kharthol toward distant Azorra.

We had been rising steadily all the time, so that now we cruised along at more than a thousand feet above the surface. High overhead was the great band of moon-dust, below us the lush grasslands. Kharthol was no more than a speck on the horizon.

Tuarra stirred and turned to me, smiling. She slipped a smooth golden arm about my neck, pressing close, offering her lips.

A flier is no place to make love, even to your mate, but I could not resist kissing my princess. We clung together, murmuring those words lovers speak to one another on such occasions. We were so engrossed that we never noticed the big battle cruiser high above—until its shadow fell across our bodies.

I glanced up. Between us and the band of shattered moons was a mighty aerial battleship, a hundred times larger than my flier. Its port and starboard sides bristled with heavy guns. Its broad, thick metal keel was polished so brightly it seemed to shine with inner light where the band-light caught it. Heads rimmed the rails, peering down.

"Who flies the night on a stolen Khartholian flier?"

My heart was leaden in my ribcase, but I decided to brazen it out. I called out, "Morr Van, panar of the Fourth Air Squadron."

There was a little silence. Then: "Rise to be recognized, Morr Van."

I looked at Tuarra. Her eyes were deep purple pools of fright as she whispered, "Even if they accept the fact that you're Morr Van, which you aren't, you're out of uniform, in an experimental flier and—"

"—and running away with the daganna of Kharthol," I ended gloomily. My hand touched the controls.

Alone, I might have slipped and dodged that great battle-wagon, but with Tuarra beside me the little craft would not be half so fast as it normally would.

I sighed, "I'm going to surrender."

Her hand touched mine. "No, Alan Morgan. I forbid it. As princess of Kharthol, I refuse to yield to my enemies."

I admired her courage but not her good sense. Alive, we still had a chance. Dead, our race was run. I told her this as I lifted the flier to the height of the deck above us. Half a thousand faces stared as we circled slowly, bumping our moldboards.

As I handed Tuarra to the officers grouped along the rail, a whisper became a sudden roar.

"Tuarra! The princess Tuarra!"

She disappeared in a clump of smiling, shouting men, leaving me alone upon the flier. I could have dropped flat and thrown on the controls to their fullest speed, but I could not leave Tuarra. Fastening the landing straps to the rings on the battleship's hull, I stepped onto the wide deck myself. Instantly I was surrounded by a dozen armed men.

An officer pushed forward.

"Where are your squadron insignia, Moor Van?"

"I have none," I admitted.

"Why not?"

"I suppose because I am not Morr Van."

The officer scowled at me. "What were you doing with the princess? Who are you?"

"I am Alan Morgan, a citizen of the planet Earth, and I am with the princess because I am her husband."

The officer stared at me with wide, horrified eyes a full ten seconds before he leaped to slap me across the face. He never made it. My fist met him in mid-air and rammed him back a dozen feet. He was unconscious as he hit the deck.

My blade came out. I was white with rage. It seemed that everything had gone against me, ever since I had set foot on Llarn. Just when things were brightening, along had come this Khartholian patrol boat, skimming above the most southerly boundaries of the grasslands.

The Khartholians were willing to fight. The dozen men ringing me in came at me as one. Steel rang and clashed.

One man went down, and then another, both with wounds that looked more serious than they were. It was a hopeless fight. I could not hope to defeat the crew of an entire battleship. But so great was my fury that I was lifted out of myself.

I fought that night as never before. My blade was three places at once, parrying, thrusting, riposting. It flew here at a golden hide, there at an arm that it bloodied with a long furrow; it slid easily into a naked thigh.

The dozen were gone now, but there were more Kharthoians in their place. My arm was untiring as it sent my long slim blade darting in and out. I was not so much a man as I was a machine. The blade was the real life of me and it seemed to act under its own will.

With the rail at my back, I battled as no man had ever battled on this planet Llarn. My other fights were as nothing, for these Khartholian airmen were picked warriors. They came at me with unflinching courage, as dogs will bait and harry a bear until the arrival of the hunter.

I do not know how long the fight lasted. I felt no weariness, no sense of anything but the sheer savage delight in conflict. There must be a touch of the atavist in me, extending back into the caveman days of Earth. I gloried in this battle. I laughed as I fought, and constantly I taunted my enemies.

Once they fell back, points lowered. Gratefully I gulped at the cold night air, but I did not lower my blade. One of my opponents, a handsome man in the ornate insignia of a korbar, shook his head at me.

"Whoever you are, citizen of that strange world you call Arth, you are the greatest swordsman I have ever seen."

Mutters of agreement ran among his fellows.

The korbar urged me to surrender. "You have fought with honor. You will be accorded all the respect we give to honored prisoners."

"What says the princess?"

He gave us an odd glance. "The princess is marked to

139

marry Gorlun Duv, the dagan of Kharthol. She is no concern of yours."

"The princess is my wife. She marries no man while I live."

The korbar sighed and made a motion with his hand. He and his fellows came at me again. But their hearts were not in it, so that they merely went through the motions. Nor did I press an attack, being content to fend away their points. These were brave men, only doing their duty as soldiers. I could not find it in me to bloody my blade in their flesh. It was stalemate between us.

Eventually, of course, I must weaken. And when I did they would swarm over me, disarm me and make me their prisoner. But before this happened, Tuarra was running across the deck, crying out imperious orders.

The korbar and his men fell away. Tuarra came into my arms and kissed me. Then, proudly, she turned to face her warriors.

"This is the man I love," she told them. "He has fought for and won me as his bride. He is no traitor as is Gorlun Duv. He could have run away to save himself. His fate from now on is my fate."

The commander of the ship moved forward slowly. He was an older man, with gray at the temples of his black hair. He bowed to the princess.

"You leave me no choice, highness. I must arrest you both."

Tuarra lifted her chin high. "If you conceive that to be your duty, Takon Tul—do it!"

As my fingers tightened about the hilt of my sword, the korbar said, "As a prisoner of state, I think Alan Morgan may be permitted to wear his sword." He added through his teeth, "He has used it only in defense of the princess we all serve."

The akkar, the supreme commander of the ship, nodded slowly. He looked shamefaced. Later I was to learn he was an old friend and companion at war of Drakol Tu. He had not relished the change in dagans that now tore Kharthol into two camps, but he was soldier enough to accept the orders of the man who sat its throne.

The korbar himself—his name was Tarr Ton, Tuarra whispered as we followed him—conducted us to a luxurious cabin used by dignitaries upon the occasion of a journey out of Kharthol. It was done in gray and gold, and consisted of a small living room with an attached bedchamber.

As the door closed, leaving us alone, Tuarra collapsed into a chair. Her lower lip trembled, but she was fiercely determined to stand up to Gorlun Duv, no matter what fate it brought her.

"You'd be safer if I'd played the coward and fled away on that flier," I gloomed at her.

Her slanted eyes flashed. "We face our destiny together!"

I drew her up from the chair and into my arms. I kissed her gently. I told her that while I wore a sword, we were not beaten. Her rueful smile was an enchantment that made me hold her close.

I drew her into the bedchamber and made her lie down. I heaped her with coverlets and made ready to sleep myself in a nearby chair. As my eyelids closed I remembered that this was our wedding night.

CHAPTER TEN

IT WAS TWO hours past dawn when the battle flier settled into its slot on the flight deck lifting above the rooftops of the city of Kharthol. Ladders were wheeled up to the main deck and Tuarra was handed down to a lesser officer by Takon Tu himself.

141

The colors of the princess had broken out from the flier as it circled the city awaiting landing instructions. The hum of talk on the flight deck and the sound of music in the streets below us told me that the news was popular among the people. My glimpse of a unit of warriors drawn up near the deck exit tempered that delight. Gorlun Duv was ready for trouble.

Tarr Ton walked beside us, saluting the commander of the palace guards. The guards commander demanded our complete surrender, adding that I was to turn over my sword to him.

"The princess of Kharthol does not surrender in her own city," Tarr Ton snapped. "As for her companion, he is her—honored guest. He goes where she goes in Kharthol, as is the law."

The guardsman bit his lip. His eyes touched the princess, then me. At heart, he was a loyal Khartholian sworn to obey the daganna as well as the dagan. The fact that the dagan of Kharthol, Gorlun Duv, was not the father of its princess tore at his every instinct.

He sighed, then nodded. "So be it. I shall not insist upon the formalities." His tone said he was in over his depth. If he insulted the princess by arresting her, he might be punished by Gorlun Duv. And he could not take my sword without also putting Tuarra under arrest.

"Follow me," he muttered.

A state carriage was waiting for us, drawn by half a dozen pure white drals. They were beautiful animals, the first albino drals I had ever seen. Their horns were golden as were their hooves, but otherwise they were all white.

We moved through the broad avenues of Kharthol that were lined with cheering, waving people. Palace guards on drals preceded and followed us. In the carriage proper, Tuarra and I sat on one seat while Tarr Ton faced us. We were a gloomy trio.

The Hall of State in Kharthol is an impressive building. It towers high above the rooftops of the city and its building blocks are of white and black marble that give a most pleasing effect to the overall picture. Twin towers flank its golden dome and statues of past dagans rim its imposing facade. A flight of wide, shallow steps mount upward to the pillared arch that is its entrance.

I touched Tuarra to precede us.

Head high she walked forward, every inch of her golden body that of a ruler born to wear a crown. I was proud of her as she moved between the pillars and under the archway and into the coolness of the great audience hall. Just so had she walked with me to face Ulazza in the city of Azorra.

In her eyes, Gorlun Duv was a usurper.

He sat the golden throne of Kharthol, arms resting on its metal arms, eyes bright with suppressed fury. To see me walking so calmly behind the daganna must have been an affront to his pride. His glance touched my sword and his lips thinned to a dangerous line.

When Tuarra halted a few feet from the throne steps, he leaned forward. "Why did you run away?" he grated harshly. "I offered you the throne."

"The throne is not yours to offer, Gorlun Duv. It belongs to my father, Drakol Tu. And after him—to me."

He sneered, "Drakol Tu is dead."

"Drakol Tu lives," I cried, stepping forward. "He lives and makes alliance with the Azunn, gathering an army of blue men and loyal Ktharholians about him to reclaim the throne you took from him by treachery."

The usurper came off his golden chair to a spot halfway down the steps. His voice trembled as he shouted, "Why does that man wear a sword?"

It was Tarr Ton who answered, explaining that I was an honored guest of the daganna and protocol demanded that I retain my weapons.

"He is my prisoner," shouted Gorlun Duv. "Disarm him!"

I fully intended to spit the rule of Kharthol on my sword

as I yanked it clear of the scabbard, but Tuarra stayed me with an outflung hand.

"Wait, Gorlun Duv—before you commit an act that will cost you your throne, if not your very life."

He looked at her coldly.

Tuarra said, "This man you order disarmed is now my husband, wed this past night in the temple of Astarra before the arch-priest himself. You know what this means, Gorlun Duv—even to a man without honor."

The usurper went white. He looked at the daganna, then at me, his face distorted with utter rage. Only one way to win this woman who faced him so bravely was left open to him.

Tuarra smiled. "Yes, Gorlun Duv. If Alan Morgan dies by any hand other than your own—I may never be your bride."

She did not need to add that he would eventually lose the throne he had taken over, were this to happen. Gorlun Duv understood well enough that without the princess as his wife, he could scarcely hope to maintain his hold on the rank of dagan. He stared down at us helplessly. He wore a sword. He could have brought it out and fought me man to man and let destiny decide which of us would win the princess of Kharthol.

He did not. His teeth bit into his lower lip and he scowled blackly, but he kept his hand far from his swordhilt. At last he lifted an arm and gestured.

"Take away the man. Put him in the dungeons."

Tuarra laughed. "Unless you put me in the dungeons also, this you cannot do, Gorlun Duv. Alan Morgan is my prince consort."

I almost felt sorry for Gorlun Duv. He was a great warrior, a born leader of men. On a dozen battlefields he had proved his right to his rank as supreme commander of the armies. There was a wide streak of ambition in Gorlun Duv, however. Having attained to alkar of Kharthol, he wanted also to be its dagan.

The fighting men of Kharthol loved him. Heedlessly, recklessly, they had followed his lead when, unknown to them, he had abducted Drakol Tu and turned him over to Morlan Az. Without a dagan, Kharthol had reluctantly accepted the rule of its former alkar.

Now that Drakol Tu still lived, however—

Kharthol would be torn by a civil war. Too many of its people were loyal to their former dagan, who had succeeded to the throne by right of inheritance, not by ruse and deceit.

I glanced at Tuarra. Now she understood why marriage to me gave her a trump card in this battle between herself and the usurper. I whispered a swift word of thanks to her father for the advice he had given me in Azorra.

We waited for Gorlun Duv to commit himself.

If he arrested both Tuarra and me, he alienated all Kharthol. If he permitted me to live, he would give up all hope of keeping his throne. If he had me killed, he could never marry the princess. If he killed me himself—

Ah, that was his only recourse.

His hand twitched toward his hilt, then fell away. Indecision was clearly written all over his face. His people waited, crowding the great hall, staring up at this man who was their ruler. Had he flung himself upon me, they would have praised him and should he kill me, would have welcomed him as their ruler.

Instead, he turned his back upon me and mounted the throne. From the massive golden chair he gave his orders.

"Imprison the prince consort and the daganna in the pits below the palace," he said heavily. His mouth twitched. "Perhaps the cold and the wet will cause the princess to forget her nobility of soul and—come to her senses."

We walked out between rows of silent, frowning men and women. Gorlun Duv had acted as a coward, in their eyes. Moreover, he had offered an unforgivable affront to their daganna. I saw men whispering to one another as we filed past. They did not like what had taken place in Kharthol this day.

145

Deep into the subterranean corridors that underlay the structure of the palace we walked. Here only faint strips of the glowing metal gave any light. As we moved along we could hear the scurrying feet of rodents traversing the intersecting tunnels, fleeing from the torches held by our captors.

I held Tuarra by the hand, though she needed no encouragement. Her cheeks were flushed an angry red. Imprisonment by the blue men had been as nothing to her spirit. But these were her own people, sworn to obey her.

The torches halted. A barred door clanged open.

The guards moved between us suddenly, cutting me off from Tuarra. Strong hands rammed into my shoulders, pitching me forward into utter blackness. I hit the stone floor hard and rolled into a heavy table. I lay there half-stunned, hearing Tuarra screaming as she was carried away.

Then there was silence.

I got to my feet. The darkness was so absolute I felt as if I were blind. I put out my hands as I stumbled toward the barred doorway. On either side of it was a stone wall, extending perhaps ten feet until it touched another wall. The room itself was roughly twenty feet in depth, I discovered by walking the entire circumference of the cell.

At least there was a cot here, and a table.

I lay down upon the cot.

Gorlun Duv had found another way out of his difficulty. He would keep me here until I starved to death. He would give me a state funeral and marry my widow. It was that simple. Like the poor fool I was, I had deluded myself into supposing he had only one way out of his quandary.

True, he had not made himself popular by his decision, but I grudgingly admitted that being a live but unpopular dagan was infinitely better than being a popular dead one. I would not have acted as Gorlun Duv had acted. I would have hurled myself upon anyone standing between me and Tuarra. But—I was not Gorlun Duv.

After awhile, I slept.

I have found that any problem, no matter how pressing,

how distasteful or discouraging, is never worth losing sleep over. If it can be resolved at all, it will be better treated while fresh and alert.

Later I awoke and lay a long time listening to the rodents moving back and forth in the corridors. I wondered if any of them were as large as the sleeth which I had fought and killed in the tunnels below Azorra. There was no khorl here to rescue me now.

Again I slept, again I woke.

Sometime during the dark timelessness, the tortures of thirst drove me to my feet. Before when I had groped along the walls, they had felt moist, here and there. I sought out those spots again, touched dampness with my fingertips and then with my tongue.

From somewhere beyond the pits, water oozed through the porous building stones in little droplets. I licked them up with my tongue like an animal. For I was no more than a blind, dumb animal in these hours of my incarceration. At all costs, forgetting everything else, I hungered only to stay alive.

Those drops of water sustained me.

I lost track of time in that blackness. A single day or an entire week may have passed without my knowing it. I rarely moved off the cot because I wanted to conserve my strength. Such strength as I had left was leaving me rapidly when at last I heard my name called.

"Alan Morgan! Alan Morgan—do you live?"

I tried to sit up, and could not. Was I losing my mind? Was I now hearing the voices that all madmen seem to hear? I moistened my lips with my tongue.

"Here," I croaked. "Over here."

I heard footsteps, the grate of a key in a lock. The barred door opened. Someone said, "I dare not light a torch. There are patrols moving here and there in the pits."

A hand went under my neck lifting my head while a container of some sort was put against my lips. I did not fear this to be a trick of Gorlun Duv. If he had meant to poison me, he would have done so long ago. But if he should poison me, he would take a risk that physicians might learn the fact and announce it to all Kharthol. No, Gorlun Duv would take no chances. He would let me die a natural death so he might marry my widow.

I swallowed sweet cool liquid that put a fire in my veins. My unknown benefactor would not let me drink as swiftly as I desired but allowed me only slow sips until I felt strong enough to sit up.

"Who are you?"

"A panar in the command of korbar Tarr Ton. Don't talk. Let me. Drakol Tu is outside the walls of Kharthol with an army of loyal Khartholians and blue men under the command of Morlan Az. The fighting is joined all along the walls. Fliers from our sister cities Khanol and Prothol are engaged in a terrible air battle above us."

His hands aided me to stand. I tilted the container of liquid to my lips and drank from time to time. At each swallow, more strength flooded my body.

"Gorlun Duv will order you executed if you are not dead within the hour. An expert killer will be despatched to make your death look like suicide. We only learned where you were located when Tarr Ton intercepted his orders. He could not come himself, so he sent me."

The panar closed and locked the barred door behind him. "It will give them something to think about," he chuckled. "When they discover that Alan Morgan can walk through walls, Gorlun Duv will have an added worry."

He lead a fast pace along the tunnels. When he judged himself safe from discovery—we were well beyond the palace boundaries here—he lighted a lantern he carried at his belt. By its rays we made swift progress.

"You must eat and rest," the officer told me.

"I want only to find Tuarra."

He grinned. "That too, Alan Morgan—but only when you have your strength back. Or have you forgotten that Gorlun Duv has the right to challenge you to a duel?"

I grunted. I would curb my impatience. I followed up a spiralling staircase and into the lower levels of Tarr Ton's own home. I sat where the panar pointed and I ate the thick steak and drank the cool liquid he ordered me to swallow.

I admitted when I was done that I felt much stronger.

"Not as strong as we would like you to be," said the officer, "for you were in the pits close to a full week. We were afraid you might have died of thirst."

I told him how I had licked the beads of moisture off the stone walls. While I ate, I listened to the sounds of battle moving through the city. High above, the detonating shells of the mighty battlefliers were causing a manmade thunder that rocked the houses of Kharthol on their foundations. Outside the walls, exploding bombs and rayrifles hitting their targets added to the awesome noise.

The panar glanced at his chronometer.

"It is almost time," he said.

"Time for what?"

"Gorlun Duv will have discovered you gone by now. He will be forced to search the pits to produce your dead body. Only under such a condition—and the cause of your death proved to be a natural one or by your own hand—can he hope to wed Tuarra."

"What am I to do?"

"Everything has been arranged. The princess will be spirited from the palace, you will meet her, and together you will raise her standard over that of Gorlun Duv."

I chuckled, "That ought to force his hand."

"You are not without friends in Kharthol, Alan Morgan. The princess had told of how you fought for her in Paloranis, how you rescued her from Azorra and escaped from the isle of Inislan. All Kharthol feels you have won the right to meet Gorlun Duv in personal combat."

"The fighting forces too?"

The panar smiled. "The warriors of Kharthol most of all. We admire a brave man. The stand you made on the battle

149

flier is public knowledge. No man on Llarn could have withstood so many blades at once."

"Gorlun Duv will have heard of it, too?"

"Gorlun Duv knew of it in the throne room when he offered you his back instead of his swordblade."

It explained his conduct, if it did nothing toward proving his courage. Kar Kull added, "I can find pity in my heart for him. The gods know I would not like to face you alone."

I rose to my feet. "Come, Kar Kull. Take me to the princess."

We found Tuarra of Kharthol in a corner of the great Hall of Dagans, surrounded by a number of the palace guard. Facing her was Gorlun Duv with an equal number of guardsmen at his back. Evidently she and her escort had been surprised as they were leaving the palace, on their way to meet me. The princess confronted him with haughty brows and upflung chin. The usurper was glowering at her, face black with rage. Had he been the true ruler of Kharthol, I am sure he would have ordered her death, but he knew too well the temper of his people and was aware that any such high-handed method might only result in his own downfall.

As our footfalls echoed in the great chamber, he swung around to stare at me with wide eyes. Indecision and surprise mingled with his anger. He looked to be upon the point of throwing himself at me with his bare hands.

"So," he sneered, staring at Kar Kull, "the soldiers of Kharthol befriend traitors."

"Alan Morgan is no traitor, Gorlun Duv," the panar said boldly. "He is the husband of our daganna. That is enough for me to know."

"It is not enough for me," the usurper cried out. "Where are you from, you who call yourself Alan Morgan? You consort with khorls! You engage in missions for an ephelos. How do we know that *you* are not a khorl or—even worse, an ephelos?"

"Were I an ephelos, you would be dead by now, Gorlun

Duv," I answered him. "And were I a khorl—I would blast you where you stand."

Gorlun Duv gnawed at his lip. His eyes went from Tuarra to me, and back to the girl. He said heavily, "The fact of your marriage to the daganna has been attested by the priests of Astarra. According to our law, I cannot marry her—unless I slay you in single combat."

I think Gorlun Duv would have liked our meeting to be somewhere other than the Hall of Dagans, where he could play no tricks on me with help from the guards dedicated to him. Too many loyal Khartholians stood with Tuarra for him to suggest it.

There was no other way open, and so he yanked out his blade and hurled himself at me, point first. Tuarra exclaimed with the suddenness of his movement, but I only leaped backward, freeing my own sword. As he came in, I caught his blade with mine, circling it to one side.

Then I was leaping forward, fighting for everything on Llarn that I held dear, Tuarra of Karthol and my life. Gorlun Duv was a great swordsman. His blade was a blur of steel in the light pouring from the high windows. It thrust and parried with an almost incredible swiftness. I understood how the usurper had won the affection of his fighting men. Had he been less ambitious, had he not set himself up as dagan of Karthol, he might have lived out a long, honored life.

I had little time to think as I battled with every last ounce of skill I possessed, yet I knew that I would never go back to Earth, that I would live out my life on Llarn—and I meant to live that life with the woman I loved. Kill Gorlun Duv, and Drakol Tu would rule as dagan. Kill Gorlun Duv and Tuarra would be mine. Kill Gorlun Duv and peace would come upon this city that was withstanding the attacks of loyal soldiers and the blue men from Azorra.

Gorlun Duv was stepping back and parrying as his left hand dipped out of sight. I was thrusting, fully extended—

when I saw his swordbelt come leaping from his middle, slipping outward like a snake, straight for my eyes!

Sunlight glinted on the buckle an instant before it thudded hard against my face. The buckle was heavy, of a dark metal. It crashed home and for an instant, I reeled back dizzily.

Vaguely I knew that Gorlun Duv was shouting in triumph and leaping toward me, that Tuarra was crying out in dismay, that Kar Kull was snarling almost at my elbow. There was no way I could thrust home at Gorlun Duv. I was off balance and he was in midair, leaping at me with his point extended for my chest.

I dropped my sword. I caught the belt before it could fall. I jerked sideways on it.

Gorlun Duv had wrapped the end of the belt about his left hand for greater hitting power. Now that precaution acted against him, for he could not free his hand as I jerked on the buckle. He pitched sideways, falling with his sword held out before him. The steel made a grating sound on the tiles as I hurled myself on his back.

My arms went under his armpits, joined behind his neck. With this full nelson hold I made my muscles bulge. Gorlun Duv grunted. His head dropped lower and lower toward his chest. His body tried to lift, to shake me loose. Deeper into his chest his chin dug.

I felt his body shudder convulsively beneath me.

Then his neck snapped.

The usurper of Kharthol lay inert on the floor as I climbed from his back to stand panting on widespread legs above him. I turned to Tuarra just in time to catch her as she threw herself into my arms.

I knew that Kar Kull was shouting something, that feet were running back and forth in the chamber, but I had no no thought for anyone but Tuarra. I crushed her to me and covered her lips with kisses.

A hand shook my elbow. "Highness, the fighting—"

Tuarra pushed herself from me, eyes gleeful, cheeks flushed. A hand went to her somewhat disarranged hair. "Yes, Kar Kull. Of course. The fighting must stop at once."

Tuarra and I went out to bring peace to Kharthol.

CHAPTER ELEVEN

THE FIGHTING stopped as the colors of the princess of Kharthol broke out on the spires of the city where they rose above the battlements. The flags of Gorlun Duv were torn down and trampled under thousands of feet as men and women crowded the walls for a glimpse of their princess and her mate.

An arm about Tuarra, I answered their cries and waving scarves with my upraised blade. It was a gesture the warlike people of Llarn could understand. With that blade I had fought across half their world to stand here this day and hold Tuarra in my arms. With that same blade I would fight for my princess as long as there was life within me.

We had little time for to be alone, however. The gates were opening and side by side Drakol Tu and Morlan Az came riding into Kharthol on striped drals. The roar of their coming was announced from a million throats.

"Come, Alan Morgan," said Tuarra. "We must meet them at the Hall of Dagans."

And at the great hall, Drakol Tu put both his hands on my shoulders and with something of a quaver in his voice, admitted before his people that his daughter owed her life and he his throne to me. "And to my good friend, the dagan of Azorra," he added, "who has helped teach me that men are better off when they forget old hates and old prejudices.

153

From this day on, the men of Kharthol and the Azunn will be as brothers."

Ten thousand upraised swords attested to his words.

There were ceremonies to be attended, a great feast to be held in the palace at which Tuarra and I, as daganna and prince-consort, were given places of honor, and treaties of peace and friendship with the Azunn to be witnessed. It had been a long day and it proved to be a long, slow night.

Tuarra teased me at my impatience to be alone with her. "It is not seemly in a consort to be so much in love with his princess," she smiled, but her eyes told me she would have me on no other terms.

"Besides," she added, "father wants to honor you, to give you the starburst of merit that has been awarded to so few men over the course of the centuries."

"Tomorrow," I begged.

She dimpled at me, shaking her head until her long black tresses swirled. "I don't know what we're going to do with you, Alan Morgan. You must learn to take more of an interest in public affairs."

"Tomorrow," I grinned.

At last she yawned prettily behind her fingers and gathering her furs about her, announced that it had been dark a long time and that if the feasting and the merrymaking were to continue into the morrow, she would need rest and sleep. At her elbow I followed her from the hall to the accompaniment of deep-throated cheers.

Side by side we climbed the spiraling stone stair that led to her apartments. Twice we paused in the shadows of the high walls to kiss and whisper those things lovers find to say to one another. Then we were in our rooms and as I closed the olthan-wood door behind me, slipping the latch into place, Tuarra told me to sip a goblet of strimth while she bathed.

I had swallowed my fill of liquids below-stairs and so I waited with ill-disguised impatience for the coming of my bride. The moments passed slowly. After a time—I had not heard a sound from the next room in so long that I had begun to worry—I went to the arched doorway and called her name.

"Tuarra—where are you? Tuarra?"

"I am here, Alan Morgan."

Wrapped in a filmy scarf she came from the bath, smiling gently at me. As she did so she passed between me and a standing torch with which the Khartholians light their bed-chambers. For a moment I saw the flame clearly through her body.

I shook my head dazedly. I was more tired than I thought! I put out my hand to my bride and—my fingers went right through her arm.

Sweat broke out on my forehead.

Tuarra still stood before me, smiling gently, but now she was almost as transparent as a pane of glass. I could see the torch behind her, the drapery on the wall, the stones of the floor.

I stood stunned, disbelieving.

Was this all a dream? Was I back home in my bed in the hunting lodge, about to wake and go out to kill the wolf? No! This was all too real. My feet felt the floor under me, my hand was aware of the hilt of my blade as I yanked it free. I moved the blade through the disappearing mist that had been Tuarra of Kharthol, dissipating it forever.

With a bellow of fury I ran through the apparition and into the bath. Crumpled on the floor were the furs Tuarra had worn as she mounted the spiraling steps to our apartment. A little further on, before a blank wall, I found a golden hair ornament where she had dropped it.

Had she deliberately let it fall to tell me where she had gone? All I could think was that some disgruntled dependents still fanatically loyal to the dead Gorlun Duv had abducted her. A red film swam before my eyes. I lifted my sword to pound it against the insensate stone.

No—wait!

My hands fumbled on the wall above the fallen hair ornament. Here on this particular block, there was a mark of sorts. My fingertips pressed it. I stepped back as the wall slid away and a dark tunnel showed itself. I snatched up the hair ornament Tuarra had dropped and ran headlong into that blackness.

The wall swung shut behind me but the light from the bath had given me a glimpse of a dusty floor and up ahead a dark hole that told where a stair was placed leading down into the pits of the city. I ran toward that hole and plunged down those steps as swifly as I could run.

Twice I came close to killing myself on solid rock where the stair made abrupt turns. Later I was to find that until this night, these secret stairs honeycombing the royal palace were completely unknown to any living person in the city. But this night, fresh air swept their turns, stirring dust, telling me that someone or something had found and utilized them not long ago.

I cursed my stupidity in not bringing along a torch or a strip of the glowing metal. Sometimes I had to go slowly, a foot at a time. At other times light filtered in from torches on the other side through cracks in these ancient stone walls, and then I ran.

Forever it seemed I ran in that strange rock labyrinth. My lungs choked on foul air and the dust swirling upward made me sneeze. But at length I saw far ahead a tiny red glow that suggested the outside world. I ran for it as might a man dying of thirst toward water.

I came out on a great level waste that seemed to stretch to the horizon. I stood on the flats to the east and south of Kharthol, those blighted areas where much of the original city of Kharthol had stood before The War. They were avoided now, though they were no longer radioactive. It was sunrise. It had been rising sun that had made the red glow at the end of the tunnel toward which I had run. Behind me, as I saw by turning, lay the great dark bulk of mighty Kharthol.

I could have gone back for help, but this has never been my way. I began to run across the desolate flats at top speed. Whoever or whatever had Tuarra could not be far away.

When I apply myself to my full speed on Llarn, I can cover ground in great leaps and bounds. I think I ran as fast that early dawn as ever I ran in all my life. The thought had come to me that the abductor might have a flier hidden somewhere in these barrens and if he reached the flier with Tuarra before I caught up to them, I might never see her again.

Kharthol was no more than a dot in the distance behind me when I saw them. A cowled man was moving with incredible speed across the parched land and Tuarra lay limp upon his shoulder.

I opened my mouth to shout a challenge when the ground darkened about me. I stared up at the most frightful vision my eyes have ever encountered. Were you to see a pterodactyl from the Jurassic era swoop down at you with its beak gaping wide, you would be no more astounded that I.

My blade lifted and drove through the air at that flying monster. I felt the jar of my blade hit home, saw leathery skin open and flap—and knew the bite of terrible fangs in my arm. I came close to fainting with pain as I felt myself dragged across the ground while the winged beast flapped heavily to lift me and its own massive bulk upward.

My eyes were misting and all my senses swam in a potpourrie of color and agony, I struggled but the great beast held me helpless. Out of the corner of my eyes I saw the cowled man dump Tuarra on the ground, turn and throw off broad leaves and branches that had been hiding a flier.

My blood ran cold.

The cowled man was the khorl, Kav Mork!

He could not teleport Tuarra away from Kharthol because it required too much energy to shift inert weight a great distance. And so he needed a flier to take her where no man would ever look on her beauty again.

A thought occured to me. On Inislan there had been no monster except in my own mind. Could this thing that dragged me upward off the ground—or seemed to—also exist only in my head?

I told myself the thing was a figment of my mind. It did not go away. I lifted my arm and stared at where its teeth had scored my flesh. There was no blood as there had been, moments ago. If there was no blood, there was no monster.

Even as I realized this, the thing disappeared, vanishing utterly. I gave a great shout and began to race toward Kav Mork and his flier in mighty leaps. The khorl heard me coming. He lifted his head and glared at me with his dull red eyes.

The ground opened under me. Faintly and far away I caught a glimpse of giant snakes writhing and twisting in a pit, forked tongues darting as their mouths gaped for my falling body.

I stumbled, but I went on running.

There was solid ground beneath me. Kav Mork screeched in utter fury. Any Llarnians would be inert by now under the telekinetic shock of what he had experienced here. I did not pause to ask myself whether the khorl formed what I saw from matter or from the deep recesses of my mind. For an instant they were all too real—then they ceased to exist.

Kav Mork leaped toward Tuarra, to snatch her up and deposit her on the flier. His face was white and intent as he saw me rushing headlong at him. Could he make it in time? Could he fasten Tuarra on the flier and snap on his own flying harness before I reached him with the sword I carried naked in my hand?

Evidently he did not think so, for with another howl of rage he tore out his own steel and ran at me like a madman. As he ran I saw two blades form in the air on either side of him.

I was never to know whether one of those aerial swords would distract me sufficiently to allow Kav Mork to kill me with the blade in his hand. Indeed, there are men in Kharthol who assure me that those blades were real, that in moments of extreme danger khorls can actually fashion reality out of thin air by their telekinetic powers.

If that be so, then the khorl should have finished me off quite easily. One blade already was circling around behind me, I knew, as I left my feet in a mighty bound. I went upward and over the head of Kav Mork and as I passed above him I drove my blade downward in one mighty sweep.

The blade cleaved his head in two.

He was falling, twitching in his last spasms as I landed lightly ten feet beyond him and whirled. He lay motionless, dust swirling about his dark cloak that puffed a little in the wind.

Sword at the ready, I moved back to him.

The khorl lay lifeless. As I watched, his body shrank, slowly at first, then more swiftly. Within moments it no longer existed. There was only the cloak and a tiny pile of black dust dissipating itself in the early morning winds.

A hand touched mine as Tuarra came into my arms.

"He was hiding in the bath. His eyes took possession of my mind so that I couldn't oppose him," she whispered as I hugged her tightly. "I—I must have fainted then. I remember nothing else."

She frowned in perplexity. "How could you have killed him, Alan Morgan? Nothing can kill a khorl."

"Cold steel will kill a khorl. They are only human, even if they are incredibly old, so old that when death finally claims them their bodies wither into powder."

She could not understand it. In all the long history of Llarn since The War, no khorl has ever died, until now. She listened with her lower lip between her teeth as I explained about the flying monster, the pit of snakes and the swords that came at me as did Kav Mork. Tuarra shuddered in horror.

"They were real—real!" she exclaimed. "Any one of them should have killed you!"

I gestured at the sands. "If they were real, the extra swords ought to be here, too. They are not."

"Maybe they faded away when the khorl died."

"Maybe," I nodded, "but maybe also they could be seen only with the inner mind of the man Kav Mork wanted to see them. Perhaps someday we will have the true answer."

She laughed up at me, suddenly breathless.

"You aren't thinking of khorls, Alan Morgan," she accused.

"Only of the woman I love," I nodded.

On the planet Llarn that would be my home from now on, I took its fairest daughter in my arms and kissed her.